FIRST KNIGHT

THE KNIGHTS OF CAERLEON BOOK 1

INES JOHNSON

THOSE JOHNSON GIRLS

*T*he sun rose in a pastoral sky; powdery blue in some spots, a bruised blueberry in others. Winter was setting and spring preparing to dawn in the village of Camelot. Arthur's boots crunched snow covered planks as he crossed the drawbridge of Tintagel Castle and made his way through the slumbering town.

The morning was warm even though the late season snow had fallen the night before. The dusting of snow covering the cobblestones would be gone by the first meal as more warm bodies than usual made their way into the Great Hall to breakfast. But for now, most of the village slept.

Arthur spied Father Bertram winding the tower stair to announce the new day. The doors of the cathedral were thrown open. The nave was empty. The church bells held still in the early hour.

Tendrils of white smoke whirled up from the apothecary's chimney. The tang of citrus mingled with the spice of cloves. Arthur saw sparks from the window as Dr. Blacwin used his magic to stir up the brew.

Arthur picked up his steps, eager for the day's events to begin. He shifted the load on his back as he did so. He'd left his ancestral sword behind in the weapons room in favor of his longbow for this day's quest. As he made his way into the wood, delicate birdsong ruffled branches, forcing budding leaves to break off and fall to the ground. Heavy blooms punched up through the dirt, breaking past the thin layer of snow as though staking a rightful claim to the soil.

There was no need for the perennials to fight. The winter would give over in due time. It was a new day. All was in order in the reign of Arthur, the third of his name.

War, turmoil, and adversity against his people were all a thing of the past. His grandfather, Arthur the first of his name, had waged the first crusades against the Templar Knights when the once-noble order fell into corruption.

During Arthur's own father's time, the witch trials of Britain had put the town on lockdown. Arthur, the second of his name, that same Arthur who'd pulled Excalibur from the stone, fought to protect his people against the religious human zealots and the cultish Banduri witch hunters.

In the past year, Arthur himself had chopped off the head of the leader of the Knights Templar, diminishing the ranks and sending what was left of the order underground. He and his men had also drawn up a treaty with the new age of Banduri priestesses and the white flag still waved between those ancient foes.

His forefathers would be proud of the work he'd done in his lifetime. There was peace in Camelot. Safety, serenity, and silence.

So much silence.

Arthur kept himself from crunching over a cluster of fallen branches in the wood. Safety, serenity, silence, and snow were the perfect conditions for hunting, and he had a very special prey in his crosshairs.

Most prey ventured out of hiding spaces when they felt safe. Serenity loosened fear in the gut of the hunted and made way for hunger. Silence gave a false sense of security that would pull a predator out into the open and turn him into prey.

From his perch, Arthur spied his quarry. The doe-white hair that covered the beast's body was unmistakable. The majesty of its silver antlers crowned its head like a spiral stair. As the creature dipped its head for a taste of foliage, gold dust shimmered off its rack like magical snowflakes.

Arthur lined up the hart in his crosshairs. He squeezed the bow, feeling the welcome tension of the weapon in his grasp. He took a second to luxuriate in the feel of the twine at his fingertips, his heart pounding at the first bit of action he'd had in this short time of peace.

The world narrowed down to just him and the stag. He pulled the string taut until it was ready to snap. All was silent, serene. He need only to loose his grip, release the twine from the safety of his forefinger, and—

The high-pitched, percussive bars of a marimba tore apart the silence. Lancelot, who had propped himself up against a tree while Arthur took aim, dug into his back jean pocket and pulled out his iPhone. The ginger-haired knight tapped the screen to silence the sounds. His face was glued to his screen so he didn't see Arthur's glare.

"Oy," Arthur growled.

Lance looked up, confusion lighting his blue eyes. He looked between Arthur, and where Arthur motioned at the empty clearing where the hart had taken off. "It's Percival. He wants to know how to win the naval battle between the Spanish ships and the fort in *Assassin's Creed*."

"I'm a little busy at the moment," said Arthur.

Besides that, there was no way he was giving up his tactics to the video game. If Percy couldn't beat that level of the rated T for Teen game, then Arthur might have to demote the knight down to the rank of squire.

"Right," Lance said to him, then he pressed his ear to the phone. "I'll call you back, Percy. Duty calls."

Duty stalked away from the sociable knight and made his way down into the clearing, searching for the hart's tracks. "The least you could do is change your ringtone. Who keeps the Apple default tone except the elderly?"

"You're one to talk," said Lance as he caught up with Arthur. "You've only got about fifty years on me."

To the human eye, Arthur looked young. Even with his thick, dark beard, he looked to be in his early thirties at the most. But neither Arthur nor the people under his protection in Camelot were entirely human. Magic ran through their veins, which slowed down the aging process.

"Why are you hunting with an archaic bow and flint arrows in this day and age?" asked Lance. "If not your sword, why not grab a sniper rifle and be done with this hunt before lunch?"

"Tradition."

That was Arthur's usual response when he didn't want to explain himself. His whole way of life was based on tradition, from the ancient weapons he carried to the medieval tunic he wore in the twenty-first century, to the code of chivalry he lived his modern life by. And it was tradition that the current Arthur and other heads of family hunt the hart when it appeared once each century.

"Is it the same hart?" Lance's voice broke Arthur's silent reverie. "It can't be, can it? It's the only one of its kind, and you eldest sons kill it before it had a chance to procreate."

Lance spat the words *eldest sons*. He was technically the eldest of the Lancelot line. Except that his father, Lancelot the third of his name, had not been married to Lance's mother at the time of procreation. It had been the scandal of the century in the 18th century when it had happened. Arthur wasn't the oldest in his family either. His family tree was also complicated.

"But," continued Lance, "there's no doe-hart for it to mate with. Do you even know if it's a boy or a girl?"

"Lancelot."

"Hmm? Oh, right. Hunting. Stealth. Quiet. Got it." Lance made a show of turning his phone off, and then made the motion of zipping his lip and turning the key for added emphasis.

Arthur slung his bow over his shoulder and resumed the hunt. The hart was easy to track. Where its feet fell there were spring blooms. Bright petals bursting from the snow-covered soil where there had been no seedlings before. Many believed that the animal was pure magic and that's why beauty followed in its tread. But there were side effects.

The centennial hart season was announced with the subtle change in the air of Camelot. Upon the stag's arrival, a frenzy wove through the village amongst witches, wizards, and the knights. Many of the new arrivals in town came not only for the Hart Festival, they also hoped to find that special someone with the extra spark of magic floating in the air.

It was Arthur's duty to hunt the hart and bring the stag's rack back to town as a prize. A gruesome practice, but it was tradition. One his father had done. And his father before him. All the way back to Uther Pendragon, the first leader of what would come to be known as Camelot.

Though the hart left a trackable trail it was hard to catch. It was ever alert and knowledgeable about the hunt for its life. It obviously knew it was born to be hunted, but like all living creatures, it wanted time to enjoy life.

Arthur wanted the beast gone so that order would reign again in his town. With the season less than two days old, Arthur had already grown tired of pulling witches and squires out of dark alcoves and clearing his throat as mature wizards and widows snuck off to corners.

He had studied his foe now. He knew the hart took an odd number of steps even though he had four legs. The hart's footprints looked as though it was dancing the one-two-three of a waltz. It would sound that way too if the stag were coming near.

Holding his hand up to silence and halt Lance, Arthur held his entire being still and listened. And there it was.

The hart's one-two-three steps came closer this

time. Its antlers looked more like a massive tree growing out of the crown of its head. In the sunlight, the silver rack shimmered golden.

Once more, Arthur pulled his bow taut. The weapon had been lifted ever since he put himself in place. He wouldn't dishonor the hart by being unprepared.

His bow was drawn, a dagger at his side in case he had to come close. It should not come to that. He'd make a clean kill. It would be dishonorable to do anything else.

Arthur prepared to release the arrow. He hated to maim the animal's perfect body with blood, but this was the way of things. Arthur was not one to buck tradition.

A crunch of steps sounded behind him. Arthur turned to glare at Lance, but the knight knelt quietly at his back. The pattern of these new steps had a distinct four-feet pattern.

Was it possible? Could there be another hart? A doe-hart as Lance put it?

A high-pitched squee rang through the air. The violent sound racked over Arthur's nerves. It vibrated the string in his hand and caused his fingers to twitch. He'd had occasion to hear women squeal with pleasure, scream from fear, and reach a sonic pitch in anger. But there was something about the sound of two or more women squeeing in shared delight that set him on edge.

"Oh look, Alina. Lord Arthur has found the hart."

"How exciting, Marjorie. We'll get to see him take the shot."

"Go on, Lord Arthur. We know you can do it."

Arthur had faced sea monsters in lochs. He'd been outnumbered on mine-littered battlefields. He'd once stood in defiance of God, Herself. But put him before witches in heat and he could do little more than play possum. So, instead of releasing his bow and shooting an arrow into the hart, Arthur was caught in the ladies' crosshairs.

The hart raised its head and then his brow at Arthur. Was the beast mocking him? Arthur wouldn't find out today. The stag took off into the wood, leaving a trail of fragrant blooms behind it.

"Oh, no," the ladies said in unison.

In the brief silence that followed, the sun broke through the trees and lit the serene scene. Like the flick of a safety latch being released from a gun, the two ladies turned on Arthur. There was nowhere to run. He'd fallen straight into the trap.

They cornered their quarry. Their doe eyes

pulled wide, preparing to aim straight for Arthur's heart.

"Was that our fault?"

"I'm usually very quiet."

"Except in social events."

"I'm an excellent hostess."

Arthur understood how the hart felt between his crosshairs. He would take an arrow to the heart now rather than deal with this mating frenzy. He'd spent his time on the battlefield, eradicating foes to keep his town safe. And now, for his troubles, he'd come home to a new battlefield; the marriage mart.

It was his duty to fall on the ax of matrimony for his people. And he'd do it. He'd choose a bride and marry and have a fourth Arthur.

Soon.

One day.

The ladies moved in as though they knew his time was up. Arthur glanced over his shoulder for aide from his most trusted knight, but Lance had taken a healthy step back from the huntresses. Now was the time that Lance had chosen to cease offering distractions on the hunt? There was no escape for Arthur.

But then he saw it. In the distance. A Hail Mary

mist. Smoke coming from the roof of Tintagel Castle.

Not normal white smoke from the direction of the kitchens. This smoke was green. And coming from the front of the castle. It might've been magical. But it was likely something far worse.

Today was not only the arrival of the hart. It was also the second annual Camelot Science Fair. Wizards and witches embracing the human notion of the study of the natural world through observation and experiment, rather than the God-given magic they were born with.

It was a preposterous notion; science in a town of magic. But he'd allowed it. It was easier than arguing the point. And now it looked like the experiment had failed.

There was only one witch who practiced science instead of magic on a regular. Morgan, the perpetual thorn in his side. What disaster had she wreaked upon his orderly town now?

Arthur half turned around to bow an apology to the ladies. As he did so, again, they let out a high pitched squee that had Arthur backing away so fast he nearly tripped over underbrush. He slung his bow over his shoulder and took off on a new hunt.

CHAPTER TWO

*E*verything had been going fine, just fine. The second annual Camelot Science Fair had taken off with a great cheer of enthusiasm. Well, maybe not a cheer. But definitely a healthy round of applause. Which mostly came from the children participating, trickled in with a few polite claps from their parents, and mostly silence from those slipping out the front door to join the Hart Festival.

Morgan considered that great progress. Especially when compared to the first annual Camelot Science Fair, which had only had five participants and no parents. With that fair, she hadn't actually had permission from Sir Authoritarian to hold it. That event had been a dud.

The second fair lined nearly the whole wall of

the Great Hall. On one side. And, really, it wasn't exactly a line, more of a curve. And the crowd—if you could call the ten or so people gathered a crowd —could easily see all the children's projects while standing at the center of the semi-circle.

Still, there was a quantifiable and qualitative increase in this year's fair. Yes, thought Morgan. This was definitely progress. Unfortunately, her marked success was now ending with an unplanned bang.

But one little—okay, big—explosion should not negate this day of success where magical beings came to embrace science. This was a huge accomplishment, getting children born with magic in their blood to get excited about the realm of science. To make a hypothesis and undergo experiments instead of simply conjuring whatever they wanted.

Magic lived in the gut. It was instinct. Science was deduction and logic. It lived in the mind.

Morgan had gotten witch and wizard children to hold still and think instead of rushing to react. She should get a medal. Instead, she got angry and annoyed glares from parents as the smoke billowed higher.

As the small crowd moved away from the smoke, Morgan made her way toward it, passing all the projects. Of course, there were the flowing volcanoes, bouncing eggs, bottle rockets, magnets, and musically-induced germination projects that came with the average human science fair. But some of the kids had stepped up their game this year, thanks in part to Morgan's tutoring.

Osbert Clarke had created a robot of organic matter. The young wizard had the natural ability to animate flesh, but he'd turned his brain toward imparting his innate gifts. Not only was the robot made of organic matter, it ate organic material for its energy source. True, it couldn't tell the difference between humans and plants and plastics. Osbert sported plasters on seven fingers as a result.

Ranulf Hughes, who was a telepath, had crafted a glove that converted sign language to speech. Being fourteen, the young wizard had taught the glove to curse. But it cursed in five ancient languages, which really—if you thought about it— was quite impressive that Ranulf knew that many tongues.

And then there was Morgan's pride and joy, Annora Godfrey. Annora had built a functioning nuclear reactor.

Nuclear was such a trigger word this century— no pun intended. The overreaction was due to power-hungry, egomaniacal, little men with twitchy, tiny fingers who didn't understand the science behind physics and chemistry, getting a hold of the mechanisms. Nuclear energy powered homes with zero carbon emissions. *You're welcome, Mother Nature.* Radiation was one of the best weapons against cancer and helped saved many a tata. *You're welcome, men.*

It was only when people tried to tear apart atoms that there were problems. Shooting a blast of energy at a reactive element caused instability. Hence, the bang.

Annora had used deuterium, which was an explosive gas. But Morgan had made sure to do all the safety checks. The one thing she overlooked was that the castle would be filled with little witches and wizards who weren't taught to curb their magical abilities.

So, when little Giles Fletcher sent a magical blast of green witch fire from his palms aimed in retaliation at his older brother, Niles, and he missed, it hit Annora's project and let loose a reaction.

Deuterium was an odorless, harmless gas. It was the stuff of stars. Scientists believed it had its origins in the Big Bang.

Morgan itched to stop and make a lesson of the

event. But that was neither here nor there. There, the children and their parents fled out of doors. Here, was a big, green gas billowing throughout the hall.

With the children and parents all cleared out of the hall, Morgan lifted her hands to call the gas back. Nothing happened. Her belly grumbled because it was empty of food. It, too, was empty of magic. Because Morgan no longer had any magic herself. It had been stripped from her in an act of heroism. But she didn't like to think about that during the day. She had enough unwelcome thoughts of it at night when she closed her eyes and tossed in her bed.

She had once been one of the most powerful witches in all of Camelot, second only to her sister, Gwin. Morgan may have had her magic stripped away from her, but the violation hadn't touched her mind. She had always been, and still was, the smartest person in the town. She just needed to think, and she'd find a way out of this jam.

The smoke wasn't harmful. Not really. Just annoying and cloying. And getting smeared all over her clothes and face. She was certain she resembled Elphaba from *Wicked* with green smut on her nose and cheeks.

She could fix this. First, she'd employ dispersion.

She set about opening windows and doors. But the smoke didn't go out of the doors. Instead, a breeze pushed it back in and spread smoke through the Great Hall.

Think. What else could she do? She had to stop the source of the explosion. But with what?

There was sand from little Benji Clarendon's project where he'd made magic sand that kept its shape. But Morgan knew better than to reach for it. The main component of sand was salt. Salt was the great destroyer, eroding most everything it came into contact with.

Think. An explosion was a rapid oxidation of gas. She needed an acid to stop the reaction. Wait. That was it.

Acid.

Vinegar.

There were tons of science projects using that particular acid. Morgan set about grabbing the volcano, eggs, and rockets. She tossed them onto Annora's project and ... the smoke immediately began to dissipate!

That worked faster and more efficiently than she'd postulated. Score one for science. She'd pat herself on the back if she didn't have green soot and vinegar all over her hands.

Behind her back, Morgan heard chanting. She turned around, and there stood her sister, Gwin. Gwin's lithe body was framed by the sun. Her slender arms raised. Her blonde hair shimmering over her shoulders as she used her abundant magic to push the smoke up the chimney and out of the castle.

Morgan had once believed she was adopted because she looked so different from her older sister and their mother. But Morgan took after her father with her dark hair and olive complexion. The only thing she received from the Galahad line were her blue eyes.

"I thought you were at the hart hunt," Morgan said instead of thank you.

"Once the guests were settled, I came back to the infirmary to check on ..."

Gwin didn't say his name. The sisters had an unspoken agreement not to say the name of the man who'd stripped Morgan of her powers. It already hurt enough that he was being taken care of in her home by her own sister, who also happened to be the villain's wife.

His perfect wife who took care of everyone and everything and never had a hair out of place. Morgan didn't hate her sister. Gwin was her favorite person in the world. Morgan just wished Gwin didn't have to be so perfect all of the time. If she could just spill coffee on herself once. Or if she got something stuck in her teeth at dinner. Or if she'd even trip coming into a room—just once. To just give someone else a chance to stand in the sunlight. But no, the sun tracked Gwin as she moved into the room to check on Morgan.

"I'm fine," said Morgan. But she let Gwin take her hand and check for injuries. It was the best part of having an older sister; they liked to fuss over you. "No one got hurt. It was just a mistake. I need to get this cleaned up before the Fascist catches wind of—"

The sound of booted footsteps storming down the hall came closer. Morgan had lived in a castle filled with knights all her life. But she knew the sound of Arthur's booted heel like she knew the sound of a match thrown to gas. She braced for impact.

Morgan wanted to shove Gwin away from her. Not because she didn't need her big sister's protection or support. She just wanted Gwin's perpetual spotlight shining someplace else when Arthur entered the room.

She needn't have worried about the spotlight. Arthur's hulking mass blocked out the sun's rays as he filled the hall. Like Morgan's, Arthur's skin was sand-kissed, a nod to his forefathers who hailed from the Holy Lands.

Contrary to the storybooks in the human world, the Pendragons didn't all spring from Britain and Rome. A branch of the family was from ancient Biblical stock. Arthur's great-great-grandfather was Joseph of Arimathea, the brother of a woman who would give birth to the greatest prophet the world had known.

Arthur's dark head swiveled as it panned the room, cataloging each item as though it were evidence. His gray eyes settled on Annora's reactor, blinking slowly as though he took in the prosecutor's case. He scratched at his beard, then his gaze found Morgan, and without hearing any defense, he rendered his verdict.

"Morgan."

It was only a word, not even a phrase. But Morgan felt as though she'd been sentenced.

Gwin stepped back. She'd learned over the years that it was best to stay out of their rows and, instead, to referee from the sidelines when necessary.

"I knew this fair was a bad idea," Arthur began. He strode across the room to Annora's reactor. It still huffed and puffed, but very little smoke escaped now.

"You couldn't have known," Morgan said. "You may have formed a hypothesis in the form of a question, like 'Could this be a bad idea?' But based on previous evidence, all data would've pointed to no."

"It's always a bad idea when science and magic mix." Arthur poked at the sodden project.

"That is the most elitist, prejudiced—"

Arthur waved her insults away without turning around to address her. "You obviously didn't take into account every variable."

Morgan went stock still. Her belly was a ball of fire. Her finger itched, wishing for a trigger to push to blow Arthur's big head off his body. "Did you just question my research methodology?"

He turned to look at her now, but Morgan was eying the ancient swords on the walls of the Great Hall. She willed one to come into her hand or simply to fall down and clobber Arthur over his raised brow. It'd be hard to miss. But he moved out of reach.

"I need to inspect the chimney to see if there's any damage from those chemicals," he said.

"It was vinegar and..."

Arthur paused when Morgan didn't end her statement definitively. "And? Was that all?"

"And deuterium."

"Which is?"

Morgan gulped, but she came out with it. "Which is an explosive gas."

Arthur blew air out through his nose, doing a perfect impression of a bull seeing red and eager to charge. Too bad for Morgan that she'd worn a red bodice today. She felt the strings of the top strain as she inhaled under Arthur's glare. But she didn't back down. She put her hands on the denim jeans that covered her ample hips and held her ground.

"I'm trying to expand these children's minds," she said. "To get them to think of more than promenading around a court or going off to fight Templars and Banduri."

"You want to teach them to blow up the world, including everything that this town stands for."

"That's not true."

"Even when you had power, you used it to advance science. The realm of humans. Scientists who'd pick apart a witch to discover how her magic worked."

"Science expands our minds," Morgan insisted. "Boiling, bubbling, and brewing is the way of the past. We need to question, analyze, and share findings in this new world."

Arthur leaned into Morgan. The heat coming off of him singed the fine hairs at her temple. His eyes burned her, stealing the moisture from the air and leaving her throat in desperate need of a tall, cold drink.

Morgan licked her lips, surprised to find they were moist and not dry. Arthur's eyes tracked the movement. His gaze narrowed. Then he blinked and turned away from her.

"This isn't the new world," Arthur said. "It's Camelot."

"Then let me go to the human world. I just got an acceptance letter to Oxford and—"

"No." Arthur had his back to her now. His attention focused on the chimney. "It's too dangerous."

"It was too dangerous fifty years ago. It was too dangerous seventy-five years ago."

He didn't respond. Was he even listening to her?

"Look at it this way, if I go now, I'll be out of your hair."

His shoulders tensed. Morgan wondered if the motion was an attempt to conceal his joy at the idea.

"You're my responsibility," he finally said.

"I don't want to be a man's responsibility. I want to get an education. But I suppose that's just as dangerous in your archaic mind."

Morgan didn't wait for his response. She'd heard it all before. Instead of standing up to him or yelling at him, she did something she hadn't done in a long time. She turned on her heel.

But before she stormed off, she did offer him one last piece of advice. "There's already vinegar in there." She tilted her head to indicate the chimney. "Just add some baking soda and the combination will clear the rest of the debris."

Arthur smirked, his expression clearly reading that he was not about to take chimney cleaning advice from the woman who'd nearly burned the castle down.

Whatever, thought Morgan as she turned and finished storming away. If he wanted to doubt her on chemistry, that was to his own peril because she was right. But she doubted she'd be upset if his ignoring her words caused the entire castle to burn down with them all in it. At least she would have the right of it.

CHAPTER THREE

t took Arthur the rest of the day to straighten out the mess crafted by Morgan. He had to inspect the chimney for damages, and then clean it of green gunk. None of the normal methods worked.

In the end, Lance had suggested using an old witches' concoction. The paste he spread over the brick worked wonders. But when Arthur asked what the goop was made of, his molars ground. The magical cleaning product was made of vinegar and baking soda.

Arthur finished up the work himself. He didn't trust the matter to the young squires or any of the castle's helpers. Tintagel didn't have traditional help.

Everyone who lived in the village was family and all on equal footing. There were no class distinctions in Camelot. Not officially in any case.

Just as the tables they all sat at were round, so too was the social hierarchy. There were knights and squires. There were witches and wizards. And there were also magical kind without any practical magic. Protectors, practitioners, and regular people.

The terms lady and lord and sir were used as honorifics, just as miss or mister or doctor were used in the human world. They might have different labels in Camelot, but they were treated no different. They all might look to Arthur for leadership and guidance, but every soul under his protection had the free will God had given them to live out their lives.

That will was another word for good sense. There was a natural order to the world that it made sense to follow. Unless you were one of the Galahad girls. Those three women had the power to flip Arthur's day on its head with a snap of their manicured fingers or a collective cackle from within their exclusive coven.

A crashing sound had Arthur tensing. He let out an exhausted huff of air before turning his head. But he didn't see a shock of defiant blue eyes flash him like a cat who'd flicked something from a high shelf with a nudge of its clawed paws. No, it was just the hunters coming in from the hart hunt, empty-handed, and laying down their weapons.

The sun was setting outside and the hunters were all coming in for the night. No one bothered with hunting the hart at night. It was near impossible to track the stag under the cover of darkness, even with magic. The animal and tradition demanded it would only give its life in the light of day.

Arthur began making his way toward the eldest sons of Camelot. It was his duty to greet them and see to their comfort during their stay in Tintagel. But someone had beaten him to it. Someone with eyes the color of a still loch on a clear day.

Gwin greeted each man at the door of the castle with a warm beverage and a smile. Gwin was the Galahad girl who gave him the least amount of trouble. In fact, Arthur couldn't remember the last time Lady Gwin had so much as raised her voice in challenge to him. But he knew that just as still waters ran deep, a calm loch hid areas of undergrowth and obstacles beneath the surface that could present many dangers.

On the surface, Gwin was the picture of

everything a witch should be. As the Lady of the Castle, she was proper and demure, a consummate hostess. She tended to everyone's needs, often before the person realized they had a need. She ran the castle so that things moved like clockwork and not a shield or broomstick was ever out of place.

The two of them got along well enough. Their minds were often of one accord. They would've made the perfect marital partners. Except for the fact that she was in love with Lancelot. Had been since they were all children. Unfortunately, their attraction was ill-fated.

The star-crossed nature of the love between Lance and Gwin was a result of the other reason Arthur would never have Gwin as a wife. She was already married. To Arthur's older brother, Merlin.

The marriage had been arranged—a better word might be arbitrated—by Gwin's mother to forge an alliance between the Pendragon and Galahad lines. Though Merlin was the eldest of the two Pendragon heirs, Excalibur had chosen Arthur to wield it. When that happened, Gwynfar Galahad had tried to foist her youngest daughter onto Arthur. But the younger Pendragon son and the younger Galahad daughter were like oil and napalm together.

Arthur took his traditional duties seriously while Morgan didn't take to her duties at all. She turned her head toward the human scientific world. Where he towed the line, she was adversarial for sport. If Arthur said go left, he'd certainly find Morgan had stormed ahead of him to make her own path. The woman couldn't follow a direction to save her life. That was a factual statement. She'd nearly died once rather than do as she was told.

She still hadn't learned her lesson. That was evidenced by the stain on the ceiling of the Great Hall. Arthur had no idea what to do with the headstrong witch. Maybe he should unleash her onto the human scientific world. Let her blow up their labs for a change.

Tension pulled at a vein in his throat. Arthur noticed his jaw was clenched. He turned from the hunters, whom Gwin had well in hand, and headed to check on the night's meal. As he walked, he ran his hand over his face to lessen the strain on the muscle and then continued the motion through his hair, trying to wipe the annoyance away. He was certain he'd be dealing with Morgan's next antics soon enough.

And, speak of the devil, there she was.

He cracked open the kitchen door to see that her profile was to him as she stood at the stoves, stirring a pot. White tendrils curled up from the pot, wrapping around her defiant chin like a lover's caress. Her rose pink lips curled as the vapor rose higher to tickle her nose. She lifted her head. Blue-eyes arrested him, and Arthur's heart stopped.

Morgan smiled; huge and bright and dazzling. It was a smile filled with so much joy and love that Arthur's heart pounded once, twice, and then a third time against his chest to get out of his rib cage and touch it.

He'd seen Morgan smile before. He was sure of it. It was usually when she was up to no good. Like when she'd read something in one of her academic journals and tried to explain it to the townsfolk. Or when she and her cousin, Loren, were solemnly up to no good. Twin pairs of faux innocent gazes would lock on him and send anxious shivers down his spine.

Something else went down his spine now. There was no mischief in Morgan's gaze. Just happiness. His body demanded he get closer, and his feet took two steps into the kitchen.

And then she laughed; a low rumble that jostled her shoulders. It didn't tinkle like a squeal. It shook something loose inside him. Morgan had a deep, throaty voice, and the sound of her laughter landed somewhere in his gut, nearly knocking him back out of the door.

She must have sensed him then because her gaze shifted. She hadn't been aiming her smile or her laugh at him. She'd been speaking with Igraine, Arthur's aunt by blood, whom the whole town claimed as their own auntie. With her attention now on Arthur, Morgan's blue eyes darkened. The storm moved in so quickly Arthur had no time to prepare.

"I'm making dinner, not science," Morgan snarled at him holding up a wooden spoon.

"Smells a little bland," he managed to say. "You might want to add some spice."

Her blue eyes flashed fire. "Domesticated goddess, I can fake. But you won't soon get your wish of me barefoot and pregnant up under some squire anytime soon."

She rolled her eyes and turned her back on him. Arthur could only stare. Barefoot and pregnant? He'd never demand a woman step back into the Dark Ages. He was a Renaissance man. But the idea of Morgan swollen, along with the thought of her bare toes, did unexpected things to his groin.

He took one and then another step back, feeling

for the kitchen door. His clairvoyant aunt watched him with a knowing gaze. Arthur whirled around and made quick strides away.

He couldn't begin to process what had come over him. He decided to chalk it all up to the presence of the hart and the magical and emotional disturbance the stag was known to cause. That's why he needed to bag and tag the animal with haste so that things could return to regular order in the town.

Arthur made his way to the Throne Room, where the roundtable rested. He needed all hands on deck, especially when he was three knights down from the six that normally sat around the table. Geraint and Gawain were still on a quest—an unsanctioned quest that was a favor for a fae princess. Lady Loren, Dame Galahad, had yet to return from her girls' vacay after saving her best friend, Nia Rivers, and the entire world from the apocalypse. Loren was the most troublesome of the three Galahad girls, so Arthur wasn't rushing her back to service any time too soon.

He marched into the Throne Room and instantly felt a sense of relief. Once this room held two dozen knights around the ancient table. Now, there were only three active knights seated. Lancelot, Percival, and Tristan laughed as they all looked down at

Lance's phone. A few of the older knights, now retired from duty, stood clustered in a corner speaking in hushed tones.

There were a lot of unoccupied seats. Though there were many young squires, none were ready to be knighted any time soon. In some cases, there were no males born to the families. Though gender was no longer an exclusionary factor now that Dame Galahad had proven herself worthy of her great-grandfather's seat.

It was another reason why the hart needed to be caught. Its magic was believed to increase fertility for magical kind. Arthur understood the need for heirs, the need to procreate. He was just a little less eager for the duty to fall upon him.

"Any news?" Arthur asked taking his seat.

The elder knights came forward taking spare seats around the table. It was bad form to sit in a claimed seat. But Lance and the others weren't paying attention to Arthur. Their faces were down on Lance's phone screen.

"You gotta check out this post from Loren." Lance held up his phone to show a picture of the blonde Dame Galahad riding a dragon.

Dragons resided in three of the nine realms that humans would know from Norse mythology. Loren was currently being courted by the god Thor who resided in the realm of Asgard. The god was wooing her with ancient artifacts and mythic creatures.

Arthur expected an engagement announcement soon. He just wasn't so sure if it would come from the thunder god or a certain ancient immortal who also had his eye on the first female knight. Arthur wondered if the first female knight would ever return to her duties. He also felt a pang of jealousy that she was getting more action on her downtime than he'd seen in a while.

"Can this meeting come to order," he said with raised eyebrows.

Lance put his phone away with an affected sigh. "There's nothing to report. The Templars have been largely silent. Nothing out of the ordinary."

The Knights Templars had once been great allies of the Knights of Camelot. Unfortunately, as their organization grew, so did outside influence. Corruption took hold of the Templars' original mission in the thirteenth century and power changed hands. The new leadership determined that Arthur's grandfather was the enemy and set the Templars against Camelot. The two sects had been fighting ever since. Until last year, when Arthur managed to cut off the head of the organization. Now all was silent; silent, serene, and safe.

"There've been a few posts on the dark web that lead me to believe a few ranking Templars are still active," said Percy. He was the tech expert of the order, which was ironic because, though he could hack most encrypted databases, he still couldn't beat the Super Mario Brothers video game. On the original Nintendo.

"What do these posts say?" asked Arthur.

Percy shrugged. "There was one post about a strange painting of a dragon, a fox, and a rooster. I assume it's a treasure map or a code of some sorts. I'll have it cracked soon enough."

The knights' longtime foes had been dealt a massive blow when they lost the Holy Grail. But Arthur knew not to trust the Templars' silence. It only meant they were plotting something new.

"They're clearly trying to rebuild their ranks," said Percy. "But it will take years before they can mount a formidable force, and we'll never let it get that far."

Arthur nodded. He wasn't satisfied, but there wasn't much more that he could do other than hunting the stragglers down one by one. That would be a waste of resources. He turned his attention to the other ancient foe of witches and wizards.

"What of the Banduri?" Arthur asked Tristan.

"The priestesses are holding to the treaty," said the young knight.

Shortly after the Templars had met their end, the Banduri priestesses had marched on Camelot. The ancient druid order believed witches and wizards were the true original sin mentioned in the Bible, and that their existence was an abomination to God. Luckily, only the older generation believed that fallacy.

The priestesses had caught the knights by surprise on their home turf, but their attack had been short-lived. Their leaders, too, had been displaced. The generation of women that remained weren't so staunch in the ancient beliefs. The witch hunters had turned over a new leaf and were under new, less-homicidal management. Still, Arthur knew that tradition was hard to break. He wouldn't be surprised if an elder rose to the helm to take power one day.

"If I may, my lord," said Sir Bors.

Arthur turned his attention to the white-haired man. Bors had been one of Arthur's father's trusted men and a formidable knight a few centuries ago.

But he'd had no sons and his ancestral seat at the table remained unclaimed.

"The hart hunt is a time for courtship and not battle," continued Bors. "Camelot needs heirs, especially from the Pendragon line. Magic is hereditary, not democratic. We don't vote who gets the gifts. And since your brother was unable to deliver an heir, the duty falls to you."

Arthur tried not to sigh. Things did typically calm down during the time of the hunt. It was as though the magical animal demanded all attention be on it as it made its grand sacrifice to magical kind. Arthur would much rather have battle action than woo women. But a major part of his duty was to procreate.

"It is still an option to marry your sister-in-law once your brother finally ..."

Sir Bors let the sentence hang. No one dared voice the inevitable, though everyone knew the truth. Merlin was on his deathbed. Though the traitorous wizard clung to life, they all knew it wouldn't be long now.

There would be no love lost in the town when Arthur's elder brother did finally pass onto the next life. Merlin had betrayed Camelot and, though many tolerated his presence, they had not forgotten his treachery. Including Gwin, who still tended to her invalid husband and visited his sickbed each day.

Arthur hadn't turned his back on his brother. Though he didn't face him daily as his wife did. Still, Arthur wouldn't take Gwin to wife. It wasn't due to brotherly devotion. The reason was sitting beside him. Lancelot's entire body was tense at the mention of marriage and Gwin.

"Lady Gwin is invaluable to me as Lady of the Castle," said Arthur. "But she still has a husband to take care of, and then there will be a mourning period ... at some point."

Tension released from Lance's body. But Arthur knew the man wouldn't go after what he wanted most in the world. Honor and duty bound them all to their stations. So, Gwin would nurse her villainous husband, while her heart belonged to another. Lance would defend Merlin as a citizen of the village he'd sworn to protect, even while he was in love with the man's wife. And Arthur would do his duty, take a wife, and begin spitting out Pendragon heirs. Because, like them all, he was not one to buck tradition.

"There are many excellent ladies here for the Hart Festival," Arthur said finally. "I will choose a wife by the end of the hunt."

As soon as he said the words, he felt as though the arrow meant for the hart had lodged itself in his own heart. There were no cartoon hearts that floated from the wound. It wasn't cupid's arrow. No, this arrow stung.

CHAPTER FOUR

"That smells delicious, dear girl," said Igraine. "You missed your calling as a chef."

If the culinary art had ever called her, Morgan hadn't heard it correctly. Mixing ingredients fascinated her. But the inedible elements were more her style, and she preferred a single Bunsen burner over a stovetop.

Morgan had begun mixing chemicals before she'd learned her first spell. Alchemy was an acceptable practice in the witching world, but not science. Still both magic and science had roots in alchemy. Alchemists were the first to group the world's substances into material groups like wet and dry, and then earth, fire, water, and air, and later alkaline and acid. These groupings would come to make up the properties upon which the Periodic Table of Elements was organized. It was also the base of any witch's brew or chef's stew.

Morgan dashed a bit of salt in the stew, but there was still something missing. She poured a cup of sherry in, stirred, and gave it a taste. It still needed something. But what?

She eyed the cayenne sitting on the counter. The spicy pepper was capped but Morgan still felt her nose itch. She clenched her fist, but in the end, she reached for it.

After sprinkling in a dash, she gave the pot another stir. Then a taste, and ... It was perfect. The fact didn't entirely please her. However, she wouldn't let the fact that Arthur had made the correct call this time to get her down.

Morgan truly had no qualms against goddess domesticity. But as a witch, it had never been a challenge. Spills were cleaned with a mumble of words, floors mopped with a snap of the fingers. Recipes were nothing but mini-experiments, tried and tested methodologies. What didn't interest Morgan was catering to a man.

All the men she knew were more interested in the size of their swords than they were in the world around them. Their first impulse was to slice open anything new and spill its guts. Which would be fine if they then dissected it to look for answers. To the Knights of Camelot, mistakes and missteps were looked down upon as failing. Not opportunities for new pathways of understanding.

Morgan knew human women dreamed of being swept off their feet and onto the steed of a knight who wore shining, white armor and brought them to a castle. But Morgan knew the truth. Armor rusted, horses smelled, and ancient castles were drafty.

"You're a ball of energy standing still, child," said Igraine. "What was it your frazzle-haired German friend was fond of saying? 'Life is like riding an autocar. To keep your balance, you must keep moving.'"

"He said bicycle," Morgan corrected.

Morgan had met Al Einstein when her parents had taken a family trip to Switzerland back in the 1900's. She'd met the failed student on the slopes and they talked about the substance that held the universe together.

Al believed particles, electrons, moved about in an invisible liquid. Morgan knew the liquid wasn't invisible. With her witch's sight, she could see the ether that held matter up. She'd tried to explain it to him, but she hadn't thought he truly understood until years later when she'd read his paper on the General Theory of Relativity.

Morgan had let Al take credit for that theory. She hadn't had much choice. If she'd tried to lay claim to the idea, she'd have outed the whole town of Camelot as witches.

But she was a witch no longer. Harry Houdini had more magic than she did.

Nearly a year ago, Morgan had run afoul of a magic-stealing artifact known as the Spear of Destiny. It was the blade that had ended the natural life of the prophet Jesus. A god killer, the blade was called.

Morgan had been trying to take the spear from her sister's jack-off of a husband. For her troubles, Morgan had been sliced in the gut. She should've died. In a way, she had.

Gone was the powerful witch. Awakened was the empowered scientist. She'd taken her magic for granted, but she'd never done that with her mind. It was like a beast had awakened within her and it was hungry. Not for stew.

"Did your friend also say 'A body in rest stays in rest, but a body in motion stays in motion'?" asked Igraine.

"That was Newton, and what Isaac actually said was 'a body in motion at a constant velocity will remain in motion in a straight line unless acted upon by an outside force'."

"Hmmm," said Igraine. "So, what are you waiting for, dear girl?"

Morgan stared at Igraine. The elderly witch looked lucid and in command of her faculties. Igraine was over a millennia old. She had visions, and when she did, her eyes glazed over and she'd spout prophetic words that always came true, but not typically as one expected.

Igraine had never had a premonition about Morgan. It didn't look like she was seeing things now. So, what was this?

"It's advice," said Igraine. "If you want a different life, then you'll need to make a move."

"The last time I did that, I nearly died."

"True. And a lot changed."

A lot had changed. Morgan couldn't argue that. But something was missing.

A lot had changed, but a lot had remained the same. Morgan didn't want more of the same. She didn't want to beg for a single day to celebrate science. She wanted to celebrate every day. She wanted to do science every day. She wanted to go to school and learn more.

Though not prophetic, Igraine's words were still life-changing. Morgan had to make a change. She could no longer contain herself. She set her feet in motion, stopping only to buss Igraine on the cheek. She left the kitchens and made her way down the hall.

She kept to the outskirts of the dining hall, which had been transformed into a ballroom for the evening's hart festivities. Morgan saw her sister dressed in finery. Gwin was talking with a wizard from another town, but she was looking from under her eyelashes at someone else. On the other side of the room, Lance snuck furtive glances right back at Gwin.

Arthur danced with Constance Bors. He twirled her with grace and ease, but Morgan saw the tension in his shoulders. She could always spot Arthur's tension, being the perpetual cause of it.

Morgan turned away from the festivities and continued on down the hall, keeping to the hanging banners. The family banners that hung from the ceiling to just above the floor concealed her as the town carried on its merriment. She'd never cared for dancing, not to string music anyway. She'd loved the ceremony of it all when she was a child. Now the pageantry of it all irked her.

The women lined up on one side. The men on the other. They took choreographed steps toward and away from each other. She imagined animals looking at the mating rituals of humans and thinking them entirely weird.

Morgan continued on to her room. She knew no one would come looking for her. The ball was one place she would not be missed.

Once in her room, she plugged in her earbuds to drown out the string quartet. She clicked a button on her iPhone. The Beastie Boys' *The Sounds of Science* blared. There would be no waltzing to this beat.

She looked at her work, laid out on the wall. It was the Periodic Table. The blocks of groupings showcased the known elements of the world. But there were gaps. Some elements were missing.

Even at the inception of the table, there had been holes in knowledge, but those holes had provided scientists an opportunity to find missing links, or rather, missing molecules. Many elements had been discovered by looking for the missing pieces. Morgan thought she knew the path to one; one of the undiscovered elements in the gaps.

She'd been posting her hypothesis online. The

problem was, she couldn't do the necessary experiments to confirm her hunch. The experiment was far too combustible, and despite what Arthur thought, she had no intention of putting anyone in her family in harm's way.

At least not intentionally. She wasn't irresponsible. She was careful and methodical. And stifled. She had to get out. And her golden ticket was in hand.

She picked up the acceptance letter to the university. She actually had many golden tickets. Acceptance letters from Harvard, Oxford, and MIT. But she'd never been that far from home. And she was certain it would be a fight if she tried to go that far.

Shortly after posting her thesis to the online forum, she'd received a letter closer to home. Cardiff University was interested in her theory. They'd invited her for a visit. And for the first time in her life, Morgan was determined to go.

Probably.

She stared at the email from one of Cardiff University's professors, Dr. Simon Accolon. He'd been emailing her regularly for a few months now. He was politely persistent, intellectually engaging, with a dash of social awkwardness in his texts. Did she dare drop the virtual screen and show her true self?

After the Beastie Boys finished their song, dropping Galileo's scientific orange. She tested the gravity and took a leap, metaphorically. She hit the voice dial on her laptop's app.

"Mr. Galahan?"

Morgan choked in the silence that followed. It was exactly what she'd been afraid of. Morgan was a gender-neutral name. In her correspondences, she had never bothered to correct assumptions about her sex. If she were going to go through with this, she would have to now.

"I'm thrilled you called," Dr. Accolon continued into the awkward silence.

He had a pleasant voice. He was British, but with a hint of some other accent. Morgan couldn't tell its origin. She didn't get out much. Trace elements she could classify, but sociocultural details she had a decided lack in.

"Dr. Accolon, I feel there's something you should know about me." Morgan's voice was husky, but nowhere near the deep baritone of a man's.

By his silence, Dr. Accolon now knew her big secret.

Morgan pressed the button to engage the video

conferencing. Dr. Accolon's face popped onto the screen.

The professor looked like a young Hugh Grant. He had floppy hair and puppy dog eyes. His collar was askew and his tie twisted, almost as though it wanted to be a cravat. He had suspenders and a pocket protector.

His smile seemed uncertain as to how wide it wanted to go. It kept stretching and shrinking. And he fidgeted in his seat as though he were unused to the camera.

"My apologies ..." he said.

And here it went. The grand apology tour. *I'm sorry, but the position has been filled. I'm sorry but your qualifications aren't what we believed. I'm sorry you have breasts and not the flat chest of a twelve-year-old boy whom we would hire over a female pretending she knew the sciences.*

" ...I just assumed—"

"That I was a man," said Morgan.

"Well, yes." He pinched the bridge of his nose, a pained expression darkening his features. "I'm so embarrassed."

And now he'd blame her for not correcting him in their initial correspondences and wasting his time.

"It's so lovely to finally meet you, Ms. Galahan."

It wasn't even Miss or Ms. It was Dr. Galahan. But Morgan's degrees were decades old, earned through correspondence. She didn't look too far beyond her twenties. No one would believe the hard-earned degrees were hers, just as due credit to women had been severely lacking in the field of science.

"What is it that you wanted to tell me?" asked Dr. Accolon.

Morgan stared at the screen. "Is there something wrong with the video feed? Can you not see me?"

"I can see you fine, Ms. Galahan."

"Then you can see that I'm a woman."

"Again, I'm very sorry, Ms. Galahan. I hope you can accept my apology and still agree to meet with me. I'm truly not a misogynist. I was raised by two feminists. One of my mothers was a chemist. She nearly disowned me when I decided to go into physics."

Morgan could only stare. "So, you still want me to come speak with you at Cardiff University?"

"Of course," he said. "We're very excited about your ideas. I think it may help us make a breakthrough. How soon can you come?"

CHAPTER FIVE

The sun rose up into a new sky calling the hunters into the wood. With the bright disk burning up the last of the snow, time was of the essence. Arthur had no plans to sit and wait this time. The sooner he had that hart's crown, the sooner things could return to normal.

And by normal, he meant everything would change. He would be married by this time next year, likely with a Bambi of his own on the way. Though the hart's tracks were clear in the melting snow, Arthur's steps slowed.

He would have no interruptions in his pursuit today. He'd left the women in the castle with activities to do under Gwin's supervision. Now that the word was out that he was also on the hunt for a bride, witches were coming out of the woodwork. More squeeing had ensued. Arthur doubted the excitement had much to do with his charm and more the effects of the hart.

It was no matter. His path was set. His future had finally caught up to him. It was time for him to step into its snare. And so he picked up his pace and made his way forward.

Snow made Arthur's footsteps silent as he followed the trail of the hart. The silence was good because the hart had sensitive ears. It wasn't the only four-legged creature in this wood. There were regular deer as well. Unlike deer or men, the hart wasn't distracted by females.

Arthur picked over the various tracks afoot. He knew he was on the right trail when he saw flat-footed imprints with outward pointing toes. The steps were wide-spaced, as though its owner had a staggered stride.

The hart, like all bucks, walked unlike does who had heart-shaped steps. How Arthur knew it was the hart and not a normal buck was the messages he read in the sky. Looking up over his head, Arthur saw that a few branches were free of snow. No buck stood as tall as the hart. Only the magical stag's rack was statuesque enough to have brushed the branches seven feet tall.

And then Arthur spotted the beast. Its white fur caught the sun. It was in a cluster of bushes. Its head bent down as it ate, so Arthur couldn't see its rack. But he could see that he had a clean shot.

It had been easier than he'd thought. He'd only been out of the castle for a quarter hour. The other hunters couldn't be too far behind as he was still close enough to see Tintagel's drawbridge. Seemed everyone, the hart included, was eager for Arthur to get on with it.

Arthur lifted his bow. The hart was perfectly positioned in his crosshairs. He need only loose the arrow. Just lift his forefinger and end this pursuit. Just a shift in his grip to seal the deal.

He heard steps in the distance. A shift in his peripheral vision told him that the other hunters were close on the trail. They'd arrive within a moment. It was now or never.

Even if he didn't make the kill, another hunter would. And that would be the end of it. And the beginning of something new.

Arthur gave a final tug of his bow. The hart hadn't noticed the impending invasion. Which was odd. If Arthur had heard it, then surely the hart's superior hearing would've picked up on it.

But its head was still bent over, grazing. No living creature cared for sustenance more than its own livelihood. Something was wrong.

Arthur moved closer. Still, the hart didn't dart off. With another step, Arthur felt a fallen branch under his boot. Instead of lifting his foot off the bark, he gave it his full weight. The crunch brought up the hart's head.

Only there was no silver-gold rack in sight. Lush black hair fell in waves over the white fur. The white fur split open to reveal the curves of a woman's body. Blue eyes peeked from beneath a furry hood in search of the source of the sound.

Morgan.

She was bent over picking, of all things, flowers. It confused Arthur. Because it was such a domesticated task. And it was Morgan doing it.

Morgan collecting rocks and stones? Sure. Morgan digging in the dirt or in the weeds? He'd buy it. But Morgan carefully picking flowers? Nope. It did not compute. She had to be up to something.

Not finding the source of the sound, Morgan turned back to the patch of flowers before her. Her white fur hood fell back over her black locks. Her fur coat hid her curves and the fact that she was a woman and not the hart. She didn't hear the approaching crunch of boots signaling a new clear and present danger.

Arthur lowered his bow. Another glance over his shoulders told him that the other hunters did not know the true nature of the creature they approached. He saw the glint of an arrow tip in the distance.

He didn't think. He acted. He ran forward, and thank God for his superhuman speed. He tackled Morgan, drawing her body to the ground beneath his as he rolled them both out of danger.

"What are you doing?" Morgan screeched as they came to a halt.

In answer, the arrow impacted the ground where she'd knelt a second ago with a decided thunk. They both whipped their heads to the side to see the shaft quiver from its impact. The feathers of the fetching bore the colors blue and red for the House of Bors.

Arthur felt Morgan gulp beneath him. His hand was on the back of her neck so he felt the knot get lodged in her throat. It was shaken loose by the shiver that ran through her body. The shiver pressed her breasts into his chest. He felt the definite outline of the twin mounds even through both of their outer garments.

He should let her go. But she'd had a fright. He should hold her until she stopped shaking.

"Would you kindly get your oafish body off mine," she said through gritted teeth. "You're ruining my sample."

Sample? Oaf? Off? None of her words made any sense.

"What were you doing?" Arthur growled down at her.

The hand at her neck tugged the skin, tilting her head back so he could see her clearly. His other hand pressed down on her hip to hold her in place. Only because he didn't want her to flee into the still present danger.

"Science stuff," she said. "You wouldn't care or understand."

"You know the hunt is going on. It's dangerous to be out here. In a white fur coat. You had arrows aiming for your heart."

Morgan's breath caught, but then she raised a dubious eyebrow. "And you dodged in ... to save me instead of letting me get shot or trampled by the hart?"

Arthur wanted to shake her. Why did she always

think the worst of him? He stared down at her while she waited for his response. But he had none at the moment.

He couldn't stop staring at her lips. She wasn't smiling like she'd been last night. Her lips were quirked in their normal smirk of superiority. But he got a good look at them. It was rare to see Morgan quiet. To see her lips hold still.

She had lush lips, plump and juicy with no lip gloss or added coloring. She wasn't smiling, nor was she frowning. Just looking at him. He supposed it was hard to frown while lying on her back. Gravity was likely working against her. But her brow rose.

He had the urge to smooth it out, to see what her forehead looked like relaxed. He couldn't remember the last time he'd seen Lady Morgan relaxed. She was a bundle of energy, constantly in motion.

"I don't want you to die," he said finally.

Morgan opened her mouth, and then licked her lips. Arthur tracked the motion. His belly grumbled as it pressed into hers. She wasn't flat and hollow there. She had a bit of give. He wanted to test that skin.

"Wouldn't it make your life easier if I were out of your hair?" she asked. "If I were gone from Camelot?"

Arthur had to focus to understand her words. He knew that Morgan had a genius IQ. He hadn't been a bad student himself. He'd earned two degrees over his lifetime. But he still had trouble following her logic most times.

"No," he finally answered. "It wouldn't make my life easier if you were gone. It would make my life easier if you would mind what you were told."

And there it was. That flash of fire in those blue eyes. It chilled a hole straight through him. So why did he feel so warm?

"Get off me," she repeated, enunciating each of the three words.

Arthur frowned at the command in her voice. Off her? He didn't want to move from this warm spot. Because he was doing his duty; protecting her. There were other hunters out there who would—

That thought brought him to his senses. There were others out there coming near. Likely already within sight of them. If they saw the two of them like this, a man and a witch alone in the woods in a tangle of limbs, there would be a wedding sooner than he'd planned with a woman he'd never even considered.

Those were the rules of his society. He would be honor bound by them. He'd insist upon it if it was anyone else caught with a witch under his protection. Morgan was a pure witch, even though she was the devil incarnate. He'd leg shackle any man that dared sample with no plans to purchase.

No. This would not do. He needed to get up.

Arthur let go of Morgan's neck. When he did, she lifted her knee. It came dangerously close to his groin but thankfully missed. Unfortunately, their simultaneous movements brought them both off balance. As Morgan tried to rise, and Arthur tried to shift, they wound up crashing back into each other in an even more intricate weave of limbs.

Luckily, no one was about to see the debacle. Famous last words. He heard the crunch of boots before he saw them.

Arthur knew the men had arrived by the horrified look on Morgan's face. The first face to appear was Lance's. His brows rose at the sight of the two of them as his steps slowed.

Arthur sighed with relief. This situation could be salvaged. Lance would know Arthur would never do anything to ruin a witch's reputation. He and Morgan just needed to disentangle themselves before anyone else showed up.

A cold breeze sailed through the air. Arthur

struggled against his instinct to pull Morgan to him. To shield her from the elements, of course.

Like always, Morgan paid no heed to Arthur's chivalrous inclinations. She lifted her knee again in an attempt to rid herself of him. "Let me go," she insisted.

"I'm trying to help." Arthur's fingers dug into her sides to help her to stand. But he was pulling her toward himself rather than pushing her away.

Once again, he and Morgan tried to move at the same time and only wound up getting more tangled. This time she landed with her ass on his groin. He felt as though he would explode from the welcome heat.

More faces came into view. Arthur's eyes were so crossed from trying to manage the growing bulge in his pants that he couldn't recognize a single soul. What his brain did parse was that it was all over for him. The hart roamed free, but Arthur had been caught. With Morgan's ass in his lap, there was no way they could talk themselves out of this mess.

"My Lady, are you quite all right?" Arthur recognized Sir Bors' voice.

"I slipped," said Morgan. "Lord Arthur was trying to help me up but this patch of ground is a bit treacherous."

"Here, let me help you up."

Arthur's vision cleared as Sir Bors came over with his hand extended. Bors had no trouble on the melted patch of snow. He took Morgan's hand and lifted her out of Arthur's grasp.

Arthur watched after the two as Bors guided Morgan out of the clearing. No one remarked on the position they'd found the two in. No one even raised an eyebrow as Bors escorted Morgan from the field. The hunters who had arrived set their sights on the ground searching out the hart's trail.

"Everything okay?" asked Lance as he offered Arthur an arm.

Arthur took the proffered arm. But once he was on his feet, he wasn't sure he'd regained his balance. Something about his worldview appeared askew.

"I assume you missed the hart?" said Lance

"Yes. It got away." Arthur scratched at his chest. "For now."

CHAPTER SIX

*M*organ looked at herself in the mirror. The blouse she'd pulled on was a bit more revealing than she was used to. Which made sense. It wasn't her blouse. She wasn't in her room.

She was in her cousin Loren's room as evidenced by the 80's vomit on the wall. And by vomit, she meant hot pink and electric purple animal print wallpaper. A poster of John Cusack holding a stereo over his head was taped over the wallpaper. A square television sat on a rectangular box called a Betamax. A lightsaber from *Star Wars* crossed with the Ghost Gun from *Ghostbusters* over the headboard.

Loren had grown up in the human world outside of the confining chivalry of Camelot. But her cousin's closet was filled with enough fashion runway fair to make a supermodel binge Oreos. From the hangers in Loren's closet hung low cut blouses that gave every man hope, strappy sundresses that never touched the knee, and skyscraper high heels that could double as weapons.

Loren mostly wore leather pants, sturdy boots, and chainmail these days. Lady Loren had been knighted not too long ago and had taken their grandfather, Galahad's seat. She was the first woman to do so.

Not because there hadn't been capable women. Witches and their powers were forces to be reckoned with. It was just that no woman had ever thought to try before. But for two generations, there had been no males born to the Galahad line for the sword to choose from. Last year, tired of waiting for a boy, the sword chose Loren.

Morgan hadn't gotten mad over that. She had never had any desire to be a knight. She'd always been happy with a beaker in one hand and a magnifying glass in the other. She only ever envied her cousin the adventures she got to go on with her best friend, the immortal archaeologist Dr. Nia Rivers. The things those two got up to and discovered in far-off places was what Morgan envied.

Morgan rarely got to leave the grounds of Camelot. For a long while, there had been too many dangers. Witches and wizards were often hunted by religious human zealots, misguided Templar Knights, and misinformed Banduri priestesses. In a cruel plot twist that no one saw coming, the citizens of Camelot had recently become hunted by one of their own kind.

Merlin, one of the most powerful wizards in generations, wasn't content with the amount of power he had unto himself. He'd discovered a way to siphon power from other witches. He'd learned the trick from his wife, Gwin.

Gwin had used the siphoning technique to save her husband's life. Since Merlin was a child, the magic in his veins was too much to contain and it attacked his body.

Without anyone knowing, Gwin had begun pulling his magic from his body and then sharing some of her own magic with him. But it wasn't enough and Merlin went Hannibal Lecter in the community.

Now, Merlin was on his deathbed. The Banduri had thrown up the white flag. And the Templar Knights had been disbanded. There was no real threat to witches out in the real world any longer.

The only present danger was at home with wayward arrows aimed at magical deer. Or the women who had the poor fashion sense to look like the hunted animal.

Satisfied with her choice of a simple skirt that met her knee and a pale peasant blouse, Morgan ignored the white fur and pulled on a bright red coat over her outfit. The leather felt heavy and warm on her sensitized skin.

She'd recently come in from the cold. Her pores were open and hungry for more warmth. But for some reason, she still felt the heat of Arthur's body on hers.

Morgan had never had a man on top of her before. She'd never had a man that close to her outside of dancing. She'd never even kissed a man and wasn't that sad.

She was one hundred forty-nine years old. But because she was a witch of Camelot, she hadn't had the opportunity to fool around with the opposite sex. No knight, squire, wizard or man would ever conceive of dallying with a witch without permanent intentions.

Lord Arthur certainly had no intentions toward her. And contrary to what Sir Bors might have thought, Morgan had no designs on the Lord of the

Round Table. The elderly knight had hinted that his daughter, Constance, was in the lead to win Arthur's hand as he walked her back to the drawbridge.

Morgan ran her hands through her hair, finding another twig from her time beneath the heavy weight of Camelot's fearless leader. As Sir Bors had walked her back to the bridge and out of the way of the hunt, he'd offered her some friendly, fatherly advice. It was a subtle and kindly worded warning that was wholly misplaced.

As if! Morgan knew eager witches who hung outside the Throne Room door before the hart season. She had never been one of them. Not even as a child when her mother had tried to shove her into the path of the youngest Pendragon.

Bors had the same look in his eyes as her mother had had all those years ago. It was clear he wanted it to be his daughter tumbling in the wood with Arthur. But he didn't need to give Morgan a metaphorical or physical push in the opposite direction. She was trying desperately to get out from under Arthur's thumb. Not that Bors believed her.

No one believed that science and learning could be a witch's true passion. But it was true. The only power Morgan was interested in was that which was contained in an atom.

Morgan gave herself one last look in the mirror. As a finishing touch, she put the rare hart bloom in the lapel pocket of her jacket. This was the second time she'd seen the flower in her life. The first time she'd seen it, had been during the last hart hunt.

Most women oohed and awed over the white blossom with its yellow center that appeared to sparkle in the sun. To Morgan, the plant reminded her of the nucleus of the atom with its inner and outer rings.

Satisfied that she'd dressed for the correct century, she headed out of Loren's room but froze before shutting the door behind her.

This was the Galahad wing of the castle. Each of the knights had a suite of rooms where their families stayed while on the grounds. Morgan, Gwin, and Loren were the only people in this part of the castle and she knew Gwin was already at work.

A heavy curtain rustled in the windowless hall. Morgan saw a pair of sneakers and a pair of patent leather shoes peek from the bottom of the curtain. Morgan could feel the tension rolling off the two hidden lovers. The strain felt decidedly masculine, while the female energy tended toward giddy anticipation.

"Don't worry, guys," said Morgan. "I'm not going to say anything."

Morgan heard twin sighs. The lower masculine sigh was filled with relief. The high-pitched feminine one hit a note of disappointment.

"It's the twenty-first century, for God's sake," Morgan continued. "But don't let Arthur catch you."

If the authoritarian caught the two lovebirds he'd leg-shackle them faster than he'd slice a Templar with Excalibur. This place was so medieval. Morgan nearly ran down the hall in her eagerness to make her getaway. Unfortunately, there was still a bit of stealth required. She slowed her steps as she approached her destination.

She looked left and right before she ducked into Gwin's office. The title Lady of the Castle might be translated as housekeeper in a Victorian world, but Morgan knew that Gwin loved the post. She'd been raised for it, and truth be told, her sister was good at her job.

She kept the castle running and maintained. She managed the shopping from the food pantry on down to the weapons room. She managed the bills, both within the community and the taxes to the human government. As well as any number of things that Morgan couldn't, or didn't care, to think about.

If Gwin ever got sick, all of Camelot would come to a halt within the hour.

Morgan went to the desk drawer where the car keys were kept. Cardiff was a thirty-minute drive from Caerleon, where the village of Camelot currently sat. Morgan could travel there in seconds by ley line, the magical pathways that crisscrossed the world that a witch could access. There was a doorway through the Throne Room, and if there was a church on the campus, she could likely access the magical highway. But Morgan preferred to travel like a human now that she was powerless.

She stopped herself. She wasn't powerless. She was no longer magically inclined. Today's road trip, if successful, would validate her life's purpose. And it had to be successful. The slice of the blade that took her powers hadn't done her in, but staying in a place that didn't support her beliefs was slowly killing her.

Morgan left Gwin's office. As she closed the door behind her, she spied her sister exiting the infirmary and closing the door of her husband's room.

It was just a glimpse, but the sight of him always sent Morgan back to that dark place. The feel of the blade slicing into her gut. The magic leeching from her body had been the most painful experience of her life. She still woke up in cold sweats from the nightmares.

In the glimpse she caught of him, Morgan could see that Merlin was pale. His cheeks hollowed out. He looked like a skeleton that had pulled on a thin, skin blanket. He was powerless, harmless, terminal.

Morgan gripped the doorknob. Her body slumped into the frame. She didn't dare close her eyes. She kept them trained out the window on the bright sun.

Golden strands blew into her view. Blue filled her vision. It was a familiar blue, as though she were looking into her own eyes.

"Hey," Gwin soothed.

Morgan blinked, looking past her sister. The door to the infirmary was shut. The empty hall was bright. Her big sister's sorrowful smile blotted out the rest of the world.

"Hey," Morgan peeled her body off the door frame.

"Where are you headed?" Gwin nodded down at the keychain wrapped around Morgan's index finger which was still wrapped around the doorknob.

"Cardiff." Finger by finger, Morgan released her grip on the past and met her sister's gaze.

"Is this a shopping trip?" Gwin's gaze was clouded

with guilt, remorse, and shame. But Morgan saw her push the front away and force the sun to shine through her eyes.

"No, it's academic." Morgan blinked away the onset of precipitation from the corner of her eyes, pulling on a bright front of her own.

She'd always told her sister everything. Not because Gwin pried. Her sister had one of those faces that anyone could trust. And they were close, close as two sisters could be.

At least they had been. Until the morning Morgan awoke on what could have been her deathbed to find that her sister was tending to the man who'd tried to kill her. It kinda put a damper on their late night gab fests.

They both tried to keep the doors of communication open. But it was clear they were often holding back. One topic that was off the table was the man across the hall.

Morgan had never liked sharing her sister with Merlin, even before he became a homicidal maniac. But her default was still to share her deepest secrets and hopes with the person she cared for most in the world. So, she spilled.

"I'm meeting with a professor at the University of Cardiff about my work. I'm going to go to school. To actual classes, not online or via the mail."

Gwin lifted her brows in that non-judgmental way of hers that still gave one pause. Morgan knew the question her sister would ask before she said it.

"No, Arthur doesn't know. And I don't need to tell him. I'm a grown woman, three times over. I don't need protection to expand my mind. It's a school."

Gwin bobbed her head thoughtfully. "It's close enough that you'll be home every night. If you plan to stay in Camelot ..."

"Yes. I'll probably stay at home. For the first year. If I get in."

"Of course you'll get in. They'd be fools not to have you. Do you need me to open a ley line?"

"No. I'm going to drive."

Now Gwin's features clouded over with judgment and worry.

"I'll be fine," said Morgan. "I took some refresher lessons with Loren."

"Loren? You mean the witch who crashed a car off the docks a couple of weeks ago."

Morgan smirked. A second later, Gwin giggled too. That had been epic. Loren had been running late to catch her ride on a yacht. She'd used magic to send the car over one hundred twenty miles an hour.

The problem was, there was no way the brakes could stop the magical punch. And so—splash. Gawain had gotten that particular escapade all on video and uploaded it to the town blog.

Morgan palmed the keys as the two sisters made their way to the front door. "I'll be fine. Go on and get back to your duties."

"It's been insane now that Arthur has said he'll choose a bride by the end of the hunt."

"He did?" Morgan croaked the words. She pounded her fist on her chest, uncertain where the burning sensation had come from. Then she remembered that she had skipped breakfast.

"Hmmm," said Gwin. "I think Constance Bors is in the lead."

"Too bad."

"I thought you liked Constance."

"Yeah. I do. Poor thing."

Gwin tried to stifle her laugh but it came out anyway. Morgan gave her sister a squeeze. Then she turned from the castle, face up to the sun, a smile splitting her face. She set out the door to begin her new life.

CHAPTER SEVEN

*A*rthur looked up to see Morgan and Gwin in the doorway of the castle. His attention immediately went to Morgan. And held.

She was doing it again. Smiling. And again, it was genuine, filled with joy and not a hint of mischief. It was filled with pride, a bit of vulnerability, a hint of desire.

What was she up to?

"My Lord?"

Arthur turned back to Lady Constance. His gaze narrowed as he forced it to remain on her smile. It wasn't a chore. Constance Bors had a pleasant smile. Nice plump lips, a tad on the thin side, but enough real estate for a man to have his pleasure. He'd never seen any mischief in her green eyes, only intelligence, compassion, and attentiveness.

"How are you finding the hunt?" asked Constance.

"More of a challenge than I expected," said Arthur.

It was late afternoon as they walked through the town square. It was a Thursday, the start of the tourism days for the town. The British town of Caerleon once hosted a Roman legion. The ancient fortress, aged amphitheater, and dried up baths brought in a fair share of tourists. The human sightseers naturally made their way into the village. But there wasn't much to see.

At first glance, it must've been hard for the outsiders to tell if the residents were a part of the medieval act or not. The town's residents wore a mix of modern fashions and clothing from the past. Young men wore dark jeans and tunic shirts. The ladies wore lace bodices and denim skirts. And then there were the elderly, and by elderly, he meant folk who had at least half a millennia on their faces. Those gentlemen donned doublets, a quilted coat of arms, with a surcoat emblazoned with their rank or social position in the court. The grand dames wore kirtles, colorful, fitted dresses worn over blouses.

Arthur saw the floating display of goods in most shops. To the human eye, the wares all rested on dusty shelves. In the schoolyard, Arthur spied the young witches and wizards practicing their spells and moving faster than a child should be capable. To the naked eye, the kids tossed dirt instead of witch fire. They leaped instead of levitated.

The magical town of Camelot was hidden in plain sight from the iPhone, Android, and Polaroid camera viewfinders of its visitors. Unless a person's mind could tap into the ley energy running under the city, they would see a lazy suburb that didn't warrant more than a few hours' stopover. The abundant invisible energy made a human's skin crawl and they were often eager to get away from it.

The medieval castle that sat on the outskirts of the village showed a sad, crumbling face to the brochure hawkers. Yellow hazard tape and posted signs warned visitors not to approach the dilapidated bridge. But to magical kind, the turrets gleamed in the sun, the drawbridge stood sturdy and open to any who could see it.

Arthur's grandfather had moved the original castle, known as Tintagel, from Cornwall about 1500 years ago to Glastonbury in Somerset, then to

Stirling in Scotland, and now it rested in Caerleon in Wales.

Morgan made her way across that sturdy drawbridge, her smile growing as she crossed the moat. Had she always gotten a crinkle in her eye when she smiled? Did her lips always curve like that, stretching wide like a bow? Had the column of her neck always been that long and graceful, begging for someone to kiss it?

"I'll bet you can't wait to mount the prize."

Arthur tripped, nearly bringing Lady Constance down with him. "I beg your pardon?"

Lady Constance brushed her skirts out, a self-deprecating smile on her face. "It's my fault. I'm trying to engage you in conversation when I'm sure your mind is on the hart hunt."

The hart. The hunt. Of course. She was talking about mounting the hart. Not ... anything else.

The hunt had ended early with no sign of the stag. The only action any of the hunters had seen this morning was Morgan's fur coat. And now Morgan had slipped his sight.

Where had she gone? What was she up to with that smile on her face? Arthur should probably go and hunt her down. But then he saw her near the grocer. She'd stopped to talk to Lance and Percy. All three of their heads were bent over a tablet in Lance's hand. Probably looking at another of Loren's antics.

"Lord Arthur, I'll speak plainly with you, if I may. I'm looking to settle down and have a family of my own."

Arthur blinked, turning back to Constance.

"I've been running Stirling Castle in Florida for three decades now. I'm the most qualified for the job of Lady of the Castle. I'm young enough to have children." She spoke with determination, precision, and clarity.

"That's a glowing resume," he said. "But the role of my wife isn't an employment opportunity."

"Isn't it? We've both been alive for centuries now and neither of us has found love. The two of us have always gotten on. I think we could make a strong unit. I'm a practical woman, and you're a practical man. I'm duty bound and so are you."

Arthur looked at Constance. Really looked at her. His loins gave a stir. She was attractive. Bedding her would be no chore. And she was right, they'd always gotten along. He knew she ran a tight ship in Florida with the magical kind there.

She was the perfect choice. She'd make a perfect wife. A kind mother. A dutiful Lady of Camelot.

Constance smiled up at him, as though she'd seen him tick each box in his mind. Her smile was lopsided, reminding him of a checkmark. There was no mischief or joy. Just quiet certainty.

He should make an offer for her. He would make an offer for her. It would be the right thing to do. The right thing for all involved.

"You don't have to answer now," she said. "I just wanted you to know where I stood on the matter."

"Thank you," he said. "That's very good of you."

Something tightened in his chest. It wasn't desire. Desire rose and clouded the head. This feeling sunk down, bringing him a bit low. He'd liked her assertiveness just a moment ago. The castle needed a woman to take charge. But Constance's firm tone had quieted after she put the decision back in his hands.

He offered her his arm and they continued down the street. He wasn't certain where to lead the conversation after her overture. Luckily, another's overtures caught his attention.

Arthur released Constance's hand and marched down an alleyway. He pulled apart the two embracing bodies he found there. The young man's sneakers kicked up dirt as he tumbled away from his paramour. The young lady slid the toe of her patent leather shoe up and down her leg in what had to be a nervous gesture.

Arthur turned from her and glared at the young man. "You were taking liberties with this young witch?"

The young man opened his mouth, but words wouldn't come out. Pure panic streaked down his face in thick droplets of sweat.

"You know what that means?" demanded Arthur.

The boy still couldn't get out any words. The skin of his throat, where a post-puberty beard reared a few hairs, turned green. That told Arthur, the young man knew exactly what taking such liberties with a witch meant.

Arthur turned back to the young lady in question. Both her feet were planted firmly on the ground. In fact, it looked as though she'd clicked her heels together like the start of a jig.

"Go tell your parents," Arthur demanded.

The young witch grabbed her new fiancé's hand and pulled him out of the dim alleyway and into the light of day. The young man backpedaled a few steps. But, inevitably, he began the slow march towards his destiny.

Arthur felt no sympathy for the young man. The protection of witches was the reason for the existence of the Knights of the Round Table. If a man dared dally with one, he would make the ultimate sacrifice; marriage. Which is why Arthur had never dared touch one. Until now.

He returned to the mouth of the alley and held out his arm for Lady Constance. They finished their promenade, making small talk which Arthur would not be able to recall later.

It no longer mattered what was said. His decision had been made. There was no reason to dally any longer.

Once Arthur had deposited Lady Constance back with the other women, he made a beeline for the weapons room. The smell of iron, polishing oil, day old pizza, and testosterone was a welcome assault on his nose.

Ancient swords and medieval weaponry dominated most of the room. But in the other corners were more modern weapons like guns and computers. A group of young squires sat off in the corner, polishing swords, laughing and joking, sipping sodas and wolfing down cold pizza.

On the opposite side of the room, two large flat screens dominated the wall. Arthur found Percy with a controller in his hands losing badly at

Assassin's Creed. Lance sat next to the knight, head down looking at a tablet.

"How did it go with Lady Constance?" Lance asked without looking up. He used his thumb and forefinger to make the image on the tablet larger. "You hitched yet?"

"What?" said Arthur. "Yes. I mean no."

Lance looked up, setting his phone aside to give Arthur his full attention. "Which is it?"

Arthur sidestepped that question and asked a more pressing one. "What were you two talking about with Morgan?"

Percy let out a growled string of curses as his avatar died in the game. "How the hell do you get past this level?"

Arthur ignored the knight's question as well as his foul language. Percy was raised in the wild. Literally. But his birthright allowed him into the castle walls. Once inside, the sword of his forefathers chose him.

Arthur glanced up at the magical swords. They had a prominent display on the wall. His own sword, Excalibur, glowed at him in the room's light. He itched to bring it into his palms. But he had no reason to in this time of peace.

Arthur turned from Percy and focused on Lance

and the image on his tablet. It was a drawing of a dragon flying beneath a rooster and a fox fighting. "What's that?"

"A piece of artwork that came up in connection with the Templars."

Arthur felt a sense of relief at the mention of the ancient foes. Maybe there was a pocket of the order that they'd missed. His fists clenched as though he could feel his sword back in his hand.

"But it's nothing," said Lance.

"It has something to do with alchemy and the Philosopher's Stone," said Percy as he began another round of his game. But he immediately made a poor maneuver and lost his virtual life yet again.

Arthur knew enough about alchemy to know that the practitioners aimed to turn lead into gold. The Philosopher's Stone was a fabled artifact that could turn one thing into another. Humans had been after such a power since they decided that gold held value and they aimed to get more of it.

But it was a crock. Only magic pulled from the ley lines could cause such a change. The Philosopher's Stone was humanity's attempt at such magic, and they never succeeded.

"The painting was done by an alchemist," Lance said. "I figured Morgan might know what it meant."

"And did she?"

"Yeah," said Lance. "It was some kind of process to make fool's gold. So, nothing to see."

"Oh." Arthur's grip loosed.

"Shouldn't you be getting ready for the ball tonight," said Lance, turning to Arthur. "Should we expect an announcement?"

CHAPTER EIGHT

Morgan didn't get out much. She'd been born after the witch trials of the seventeenth century. The scab of anxiety and distrust was still festering in her community.

The residents of Camelot had hunkered down in their city as religious zealots burned innocent human women at the stake or anchored them down in deep pools of water. In some cases, they'd treated them leniently with shaming in the town square. In other instances, they'd simply mutilated the wayward females.

The Knights of Camelot had formed a manly shield around the witches under their care. For a long time, no one got in and no one got out of

Camelot. In some ways, the zealotry of the knights had oppressed the witches in their care.

In any case, Morgan hadn't seen much of the world before she was a century old. And it didn't look like it had changed much since the time of the witch trials. The only difference was that the aggressors wielded two-ton vehicles instead of pitchforks. So now, a lot of the aggression was aimed at females behind the wheel.

The women might've driven too slow. Her car might've been too flashy or more expensive than his. There may have been more than one female in the car. Or she could've been too old for their liking.

Honks ripped through the air. Windows rolled down and offensive digits were raised. Exhaust fumes growled as men sped too close to, or around and past, the feminine offenders who dared brave the asphalt.

No cars collided. No engines got torched. But it looked to Morgan as though not much had changed in the last two centuries.

She navigated the hectic highways with ease. Seventy miles per hour was nothing to someone who rode enchanted horses across the moors. The Arabians of Camelot reached such high speeds that it felt like the rider flew on their backs. The honks of angry drivers were nothing to a woman who awoke to the sounds of jousts and swordplay in her backyard.

Morgan made it to the campus of Cardiff University without incident. She was glad to be free of the honking and angry drivers. Still, next time she might ride a horse to Cardiff. Or take her sister up on her offer to open a ley line.

No. Strike that. This was her next phase of life. If she got accepted to the university, she would do this all the human way; rush hour, congestion, and road rage included.

Stepping out of her car, Morgan headed toward the brick and mortar of the old educational institution and marveled. She'd grown up with spires and stained glass windows. But there was something about a college campus that dimmed the architectural wonders of the witching world. Standing in this place of knowledge where learning was everyone's pursuit, she never wanted to leave.

Morgan breathed in the scent of fresh cut grass along with the rolled up and smoking variety. A line snaked out from a mobile coffee truck. The smell of caffeine overpowered the fumes from the truck's exhaust.

She dodged to the side of students hurrying to

class. She sidestepped those lounging on walkways. Her boots crunched over a heap of snow shoved off to the side. Beside her, a guy in a t-shirt and pajama bottoms gave her a wink before ducking into the Liberal Arts building.

Finally, she found the Science Building. It was tucked at the far corner of the campus and surrounded by trees and a small manmade pond. It was the picture of man and nature living in harmony. Morgan had a very good feeling as she walked through the doors.

"Ms. Galahan?"

Morgan turned, expecting a hulking mass of a man with such a husky sounding voice. But the man before her was slight. Tall, but reedy. Sturdy, but thin. There was still the lanky awkwardness about him in person, but he looked smart. It wasn't just the glasses, or the tweed blazer, or the pressed slacks and worn loafers. There was an air of intelligence about him, and intelligence had always attracted Morgan.

"Doctor Accolon?"

It took him a second, but he nodded. His gaze had been fastened to her. A hint of surprise on his brow as he took her in.

Morgan ran a self-conscious hand over her skirt.

Was it not collegiate enough? Did she look entirely out of place, out of this century, out of her depth?

"I'm so sorry for staring," said Accolon. "The camera didn't do you justice."

Morgan started. While she knew she was attractive, she did have the Galahad genes, after all, she'd rarely—no, never—been told as much to her face by a member of the opposite sex. The men of Camelot only made overtures to girls they planned to marry, and everyone knew Morgan had no interest in that particular institution. So, no man, squire, or knight had ever bothered to compliment her.

"Oh no," groaned Accolon. "I've gone and insulted you again."

"No. Not an insult at all. Thank you. Thank you very much, Dr. Accolon."

"Please, call me Simon."

"Then you must call me Morgan."

"It's nice to finally meet you face to face, Morgan."

Morgan held out her hand for him to kiss. Simon grasped it and gave it a firm shake. Then they both let go and fidgeted.

Morgan tugged at the strap of her purse. Simon ran his hand over the locket on a chain around his neck. The locket was the dull shade of gray with bits of sparkling specks that told Morgan it was lead.

It was an interesting locket. She wondered if he wore it for symbology? The metal was related to both death and transformations in the field of alchemy. But Morgan didn't have a chance to ask.

"My office is just in here," he said at last.

She followed him into a small hole in the wall. A large metallic desk took up most of the space. There were posters of the Periodic Table, a few white-haired scientists, a candid shot of Stephen Hawking, Bill Nye, and Neil deGrasse Tyson posed as though they were a rap group. But it was the painting on the wall that caught Morgan's attention. It was the second time she'd seen it today.

The image was of a fox eating a rooster. There was a mountain in the distance and a dragon flying in the foreground.

"You have an interest in alchemy?" she asked.

"Why would you say that?"

"Your print of the *Flying Red Dragon*. It's one of Valentine's Ciphers."

Basil Valentine, not his real name, believed he'd uncovered the formula to the Philosopher's Stone. But of course, he hadn't spelled out his formula. He'd put the process into puzzles; twelve puzzle pieces which described the steps to creating the stone. The painting was one of the pieces.

Simon smiled, tilting his head. His glasses slipped to the edge of his nose as he did so. "Alchemy is a bad word in the scientific community."

"Yet you have the painting of a key to the Philosopher's Stone on your wall."

"Most people don't know what it is," he said, looking at her with renewed interest.

Lance and Percy hadn't known either. They just knew it had something to do with alchemy, and Morgan was the town resident who knew most about the ancient practice. Most wizards and witches skipped over the human practice in favor of the magic that ran through their veins.

"It's really an easy puzzle," said Morgan. "You have the rooster, which represents gold because it rises at dawn. The fox represents acid. If you add acid to the gold, the gold dissolves. Hence the fox eating the rooster."

"But the rooster also eats the fox," said Accolon as he picked up the mantle. "Meaning you could distill the liquid and the gold would reappear."

It was basic transmutation; changing the composition of one thing to make it into another. Much like adding ingredients together to make a soup. Or distilling a compound to get to its original components.

"We're basically doing the same thing with crafting a new element," said Morgan.

He nodded, excitement now shining past his glasses. "Did you know that in Arabic, alchemy means the secret within you."

She did know that. There were many in Camelot who were from the Holy Lands. You could still hear ancient Arabic spoken in the Great Hall during meal times.

"Do you think it's possible?" asked Accolon.

"What?"

"Transmutation?"

Morgan knew that transmutation was possible. It was called magic in her world. It was practiced out in nature with ley energy beneath her feet. Physical objects could contain ley energy. Morgan knew that as evidenced by the scar on her belly. A simple object had collected ley energy and ripped the magic from her.

"Do you mean turning lead into gold?" She answered his question with one of her own. "The ability to rearrange elements at the molecular structure? If it's not, then you and your colleagues are wasting a lot of time and money."

A laugh burst from Simon, as though he was the last person to expect the sound to come out of him. He looked at her with curiosity and wonder. Then he held out his arm in front of her.

Morgan made to take it, to place her hand in the crook of his elbow as was the custom in her town. But Simon's hand continued in an arc. He wasn't offering his arm. He was showing her the way he wanted her to walk. It was through another door in the corner of his office.

"We're just in here," he said.

"We?"

"Yes, of course. The Department Chair and the professors on the Admissions Board wanted to hear your presentation as well."

Presentation? Wasn't this just a chat between the two of them? Maybe a tour of the labs? Perhaps a cup of tea as they talked about enrollment?

A fine sheen of sweat broke out at the base of Morgan's neck. She was still close to the doorway. But it was too late to turn back now.

Dr. Accolon opened another door. Inside, the quiet hum of conversation ceased as the occupants realized they were not alone. As a unit, the group, all men, all white-haired Europeans, turned to look at her.

Morgan gulped. Then she chided herself for gulping. She'd faced down a brood of Banduri huntresses. She'd gone toe to toe with a psychopathic wizard. She stood up to Arthur on a daily basis. A group of mortal men, she could handle.

She took one step and then another into the room. She looked beyond the men, and what she saw had her feet eager to run. Just beyond the table where the men sat was a glass window looking into a lab. Just beyond the glass was what Morgan wanted most in the world.

A cyclotron.

It was like walking into a dream. In fact, she walked past the assembled men and pressed her nose to the glass to look at the device. As she did so, the rare and precious flower in her lapel was crushed against the glass surface.

The cyclotron was a large circle of metal and wires. Electricity flashed at intervals from within. It took up the space of a small gymnasium, about the size of the dining hall back at Camelot.

The cyclotron was a particle accelerator. It was used to separate elements. Scientists would bombard known elements, throwing them at one another at high speeds in the hopes that two elements collided. If two elements stuck together, they would form a new element by force.

It was how they planned to find the newest element on the Periodic Table, Element 119. That element would begin a whole new row on the table.

Beside the room that housed the accelerator, was what Morgan could only describe as a control room. A beep sounded from the console of buttons and sliders and controls. A series of red and yellow LED lights flashed.

"What is that?" asked one of the white-haired men. "Has a collision occurred? Have we achieved fusion?"

Simon rushed to the control panel. He tore off his glasses, like Clark Kent turning into a nerdy Superman. He bent over and stared at the readings.

Morgan's heart pounded in her chest as she waited. Her breath baited along with the other scientists in the room. She stepped away from the window and toward Simon aiming to see over his shoulder. But the moment she did, the alarm stopped and the lights went dark. Whatever had happened, she'd missed it.

"False alarm," sighed Simon. His sigh settled like a heavy fog around the room. "It happens from time to time. We've been at this for two months now and nothing. Which is why we are excited about your theory, Ms. Galahan."

Right. Her theory. These men had the idea to fire a beam to force two elements together to forge something new and wait to watch for a connection. Morgan had a different idea.

"Instead of watching for the collision and waiting to take a picture of the union which would happen in a fraction of a second, I believe the best course of action would be to read the debris left behind. A clear radioactive signature will be emitted that would prove the existence."

Kinda like a blue light to a hotel top sheet.

When she was a girl and she'd looked into a microscope, she'd seen atoms. She'd seen the arrangement of what would come to be called protons and electrons. The bright particles of light had danced in circles. They were the most beautiful thing she'd ever seen, and she couldn't understand why no one else saw them.

Finally, in 1869 a Russian chemist, Dimitri Mendeleev, began arranging the known elements by their atomic mass. The structure that he proposed Morgan knew to be true because she'd seen the arrangement of particles with her own eyes. Mendeleev by no means listed all of the elements and had left many gaps in his table, postulating that more would be found in the future.

By the 1940's they were up to 92 elements having found what they thought were all the natural elements. Then they looked closer and saw the heavier elements.

In the 50's, the scientists had come inside from the natural world and elements were now found in sterile laboratories. They were up to 118 as of now. She'd watched for decades as human scientists fumbled about a world they needed glasses to see where she could see clearly. She ached to nudge them into the right direction, but she had to remain mute to protect her kind.

And then she'd lost her sight.

The atom became invisible to her when she lost her magic. She was now just like any other human. The only thing that would allow her access to that magical world now was the cyclotron.

Morgan turned back to the men she had to impress to gain access to her new future. Why did her life always hang in the hands of men?

"Gentlemen, now that the excitement is over, and I've explained my theory, I'm hoping we can get along with my entrance interview?"

The gray-haired men looked at one another.

Then collectively, they all turned to look at Simon. He'd returned his glasses to his face, Superman once again the mild-mannered Clark Kent.

"Ms. Galahan," said Dr. Accolon, "I fear there's been a misunderstanding. We're not interested in you attending as a student. I'm interested in bringing you on my team, in search of Element 119. The decision has been made. This is all a formality. We want you to conduct your research here."

CHAPTER NINE

"How will you do it? Will you get down on one knee? Did you hide something in her food? That's always risky."

Arthur turned his head away from Percy, the pervasive knight. Once his face was hidden he twisted his lip. Because he'd forgotten to bring the ring for the proposal.

"If it were me, I'd do it on a jumbotron television screen like they do in stadiums," Percy continued.

Arthur wasn't one to make a spectacle of himself. He had a plan. He would go in and ask her father first. And once he was assured of the male's agreement, he'd pull Lady Constance aside and do the asking in private. It was the promise that was important, not the ring.

"Regardless of how you do it, things change when men get married," said Percy. "Mark my words, as soon as your legs are shackled, she won't let you go on quests. There will now be an official Guy's Night Out instead of hanging out any day of the week. And, worst of all, the meat to vegetable ratio will change on your plate, and not in favor of the meat."

"None of that will happen," insisted Arthur.

Percy rolled his eyes. Beside him, Lance didn't answer. Glancing over his shoulder, Arthur caught sight of Tristan's grimace.

The four knights marched down the hall side by side as they'd done for years. Down the hall, in battle, in triumph.

"She's a woman," said Percy. "When you turn a woman into a wife they become a completely different creature. Almost as though they were a caterpillar. The wedding is the chrysalis. And then after the wedding night, they emerge into a butterfly. It looks beautiful, but they'll wreak havoc on your garden, aka your food supply. Do you see how this all lines up?"

Lance reached around and smacked Percy on the backside of his head. Percy jerked, ready to fight. But they turned a corner and came before other people. So they cooled the antics.

Gwin stood at the entrance to the hall. She spoke quietly with Lady Constance. Arthur's gaze skimmed over the two women and continued on around the room. He told himself he was getting the lay of the land. But when his eyes didn't spot a dark head of hair with a defiant blue gaze, he gave up his surveillance.

"What does your marriage mean for Lady Gwin?" asked Lance. He'd aimed for casual, but completely overshot.

"She'll remain Lady of the Castle so long as she's still married to the eldest son," said Arthur.

"And when Merlin ... when Lady Gwin becomes a widow?"

"Then Lady Gwin will be free to do as she pleases. To take on a new role. A new job. A new husband."

Lance's features didn't change, but Arthur felt the change in his friend. The other man practically vibrated with emotion. "Well, let's get this over with."

The knights advanced as a unit. But instead of leading the charge, Arthur held back. "I'll only be a moment."

The other three knights exchanged knowing glances, but they said nothing. Arthur didn't have cold feet. He always took a moment to prepare before rushing into battle.

And this was a battle. Aside from his men, no one inside the Great Hall knew of his plan. Sure, most suspected his choice would be Lady Constance. It made sense.

So, he should march in there and get it over with. Percy was wrong. Nothing would change. His job was to hang out with the guys on a daily basis as they protected their people. He had no problem with vegetables. And as more squires came of age it was only logical that he went on fewer quests.

Everything was happening as it was intended. It was the natural course of things. He just needed to step into the room. Instead, he stepped behind the long hanging banner of his family.

The great banner hung from the ceiling that led into the Great Hall from a side entrance. The banners of every great family in Camelot hung as well, forming a curtained wall that separated the hall from the wall. If he followed the wall, it would lead to a set of stairs that spilled into the living quarters.

Arthur remembered sneaking down from his

bedroom and peeking through these flags as a kid. He'd watched his grandparents and his parents at a similar event. The two men had whirled and twirled their wives all night, huge grins never leaving their faces.

Though Camelot was a town that prided itself on family-friendly events, balls and grand parties were the affairs of adults. Arthur had always assumed he'd be dancing with his wife during an event like this after putting his kids to bed. But in all his years, he had yet to meet a woman he'd wanted to pull into his arms at a ball and dance into the night.

The music had started and a few couples were dancing, including the couple he'd pushed into marriage earlier this day. The lad wore a smile as he looked down at his intended. All traces of fear gone. They were in love.

Arthur remembered his own father had looked at his mother the same way; as though the sun rose on her face. His grandfather had looked at his grandmother the same, too. With utter devotion.

Arthur knew love was real. He believed wholeheartedly in it. But he'd never experienced it himself.

He was a man who lived in a world of magic. He'd seen the spiritual spell that true love cast with his own eyes. He was religiously devout, even before he'd seen God in the flesh. He trusted the bounds of loyalty, never doubting a fellow knight. But love was an experience that had not blessed its light of truth upon him.

He chided himself to think that that had been the reason he'd held out on marriage for so long. He was still hoping for love. From behind the flag of his forefathers, he looked again at Constance.

She was lovely and kind. His loins stirred as any red-blooded man's would. Still, he felt nothing in his heart. But he couldn't wait forever. He had a duty to perform and now was the time. He would make her a good husband, and she would make him a good wife.

Arthur took a step forward but stopped. A flash of darkness caught his eye. Something else was moving behind the banners. Or rather someone.

Dark tresses skimmed the edges of the flags. A flash of blue eyes peeked between the fabric. As she came nearer to him, Arthur's heartbeat increased, his mouth watered, his adrenaline pumped up.

Morgan moved at the edges of the room like she didn't want to be seen. Her shape came into view. She was dressed like a 21st-century woman, her curves on full display. That wasn't what tightened his body. She was glowing.

Morgan was smiling again. The look of pure joy and happiness. What was she up to?

"Morgan?"

She halted. The moment she saw him her smile dropped, as though it clattered to the floor. He stopped in front of her, wanting to reach out and catch it, but unsure how to.

"Where have you been?" he demanded, his voice gruffer than he meant for it to be.

"Cardiff." Morgan squirmed. "At a school. The university."

She began to brighten again at those words. Arthur knew she loved learning, always had. Morgan had had her head in books, her hand in the dirt, while other witches were casting spells.

"You went alone?"

"It's not dangerous," she said. "It's a school. The worst that could've happened was I'd get into a philosophical debate."

Arthur could imagine worse. He suspected there was more to the story as he watched her fidget. Morgan only ever fidgeted when she was uncertain of herself. All three Galahad girls were the most self-assured witches he'd ever known.

"The science department is interested in one of my theories of matter." Her fidgeting ceased. Her eyes lit up as she spoke. Her lips tugged upward in joy.

"Well," he said, "you are a brilliant woman."

Morgan tilted her head up and looked at him. The motion was small, but he felt something shift inside him as her eyes widened. "You think I'm brilliant?"

Arthur's heart stopped. He had to force air into his lungs before he could get out any words. "I know you're stifled here, Morgan. I just want to protect you. I want you to be safe."

He watched her throat as she swallowed. Those blue eyes burned as though she were trying to find her way to the heart of the matter. Then she blinked and her gaze cooled.

"You can't learn anything new from a point of stasis," she said. "You would never make a breakthrough. There needs to be agitation, commotion."

Arthur grinned. "Am I the stasis in this equation?"

"Depends," she said. "Am I the agitation?"

They stared at each other. They'd been in this position before. But he'd always been wary of what was going on in her head, knowing retaliation was coming. It was likely coming now since she obviously thought they were at odds. But he felt no animosity toward her. He felt … he wasn't sure what this was?

His gaze shifted. Above her head, between two flags, hung a bundle of hart flowers. A sprinkle of gold dust rained down on her head, leaving a shimmer atop her dark hair.

"I'll get out of your way," said Morgan. "You're headed in to announce your engagement. I don't want to ruin it. We can talk later."

She turned to go. As she turned on her heel, the feeling—whatever it was—seeped away. It was as though the sun was setting and clouds were moving into a dark night.

"Morgan. Wait."

Arthur reached out and grabbed her. He'd grabbed her mid-step and she lost her footing. To prevent her from falling, he yanked her to him, and she came crashing into his chest.

And now they were chest to chest. Their mouths were inches away from each other. Their lips and noses were like puzzle pieces waiting to be slid into place.

Morgan's chest pressed into his reminding him of

lounging on a beach blanket under the noon sun. Her hand on his bicep was the sun sneaking in behind closed curtains in the early morning. Her breath on his lips was the taste of sun-warmed tea in the afternoon.

They both yanked away from each other, taking a step back. There was a halt in the music and a ripping sound tore through the air. The next thing Arthur knew, cloth was raining down over his head. He pulled Morgan back to him as they were covered in a large, heavy cloth, the flag of his family.

They tumbled to the floor, a tangle of limbs and fabric. With one hand, Arthur strove to shield Morgan. With the other hand, he moved aside the fabric, trying to gain his own freedom.

The rip had been loud, but the collective gasp that tore through the hall was positively deafening. Every pair of eyes in the village were on them as they lay, his body on top of hers, in a tangle on the floor.

"Well that's one way to ask a lady to marry you," said Percy.

CHAPTER TEN

*M*organ couldn't decide where to stare. At the crowd of people staring disbelieving at her. At her sister who was as dumbfounded as she was. At Igraine who seemed to be the only person smiling as though a surprise she'd been waiting decades to unveil was finally revealed. Or at the large knight looming over her who wasn't looking at her in disbelief at the conundrum they found themselves in. As Arthur helped her to her feet, he looked at her with resignation.

Morgan decided that her best bet would be to close her eyes. None of this could be real. Either she was dreaming or she was drunk.

Drunk made the most sense. She had a bottle of

hooch in her bag to celebrate. Half of the contents were to drink; the other half would be for later to use in distilling some chemicals.

But the bottle of dark liquid was unopened. Maybe the fumes had seeped into her brain? But that wouldn't have been enough to make her drunk.

So that left a dream. But this couldn't be a dream. Dreams were the wishes your heart wanted to make true. She didn't have a heart's wish. She only had logical thoughts.

Her dreams were orderly equations aligning into solutions. Her fantasies were of chemical compounds joining to form a new element. She had never been one of those girls to dream of bagging a knight of her own. While the other young witches played with dolls or practiced their spells, Morgan had mixed chemicals and memorized the Periodic Table. Being caught in a knight's embrace wasn't a dream. It was her worst nightmare.

Well, maybe not her worst. She did sometimes dream of the platypus. That animal simply made no sense and its arrival into her perfectly ordered dreams always caused her to jerk awake. Seriously, what was the Creator thinking with that one?

Tonight Morgan had come home through the kitchens because she'd had no desire to attend the grand ball. She hated all this ceremony. And her presence wasn't necessary.

Arthur was sure to pick Lady Constance to marry. The two of them together made sense. Both of them were age appropriate, having been on this earth for two centuries. Both of them were pillars of their community who put duty over all else.

Morgan wasn't any of those things. She wanted to eventually leave this town and devote her life to science. Whatever was happening right now, dream or drunkenness, made no logical sense. She was sure it would be cleared up in a matter of moments.

Morgan tried to take a step back. But she couldn't. Something was holding on to her. Or rather, someone.

Arthur.

Why was he holding on to her? This was the first time Morgan could even remember Arthur touching her. Through all of their confrontations, he'd never laid a hand on her. Even though she was sure he wanted to strangle her more times than naught.

But of course, he wouldn't harm her. He was a knight. She was a witch—even without powers. Witches were untouchable. Literally. Both in aspects of violence, as well as in aspects of carnal activity—unless you intended marriage.

So, why wouldn't Arthur stop touching her?

He wasn't squeezing the life out of her. He was holding her gently, carefully, but securely like he didn't want her to get away.

He was looking at her inquisitively like he was trying to solve a puzzle. It wasn't the way he normally looked at her like he was trying to figure out what she'd done wrong.

His features weren't pinched. His eyes were dark, but not burning with a raging fire. They were smoldering, as though trying to build something new.

She and Arthur had had a strange moment behind the flags. It had felt almost intimate, the way he'd held her, the way he'd looked at her. As though he'd wanted to kiss her.

But that was preposterous. He was Arthur. She was Morgan. Their names didn't belong in a sentence together.

"Will you?" Arthur said.

"Will I what?" she asked.

"Will you marry me?"

Morgan's heart stopped at those words. Her senses left her. Something fluttered in her belly.

Her belly never fluttered unless she was hungry. Fluttering was a sign of malnourishment or dehydration due to an imbalance in electrolytes or the lack of fluids for the proper functioning of the organs and nervous systems. Those poor conditions caused spasms in the abdominals which translated into a feeling of fluttering.

But Morgan had eaten on the way home, stopping at a fast food drive-through. It had taken only moments for her order to be made ready, as opposed to cooking all day in the kitchens with fresh ingredients. The greasy, chemically processed food was pure magic. But it did weigh heavy on the drive home.

So, maybe it was all the grease that was causing the sensations in her belly. Those chemicals could have an effect, especially for a body unused to highly processed foods.

Now that she'd started searching for answers to the problem before her, her brain wouldn't turn off in its efforts to find the right answer.

Abdominal fluttering was also the sign of pregnancy. But no! That was definitely not her condition since sex had to be had at least once to invoke that.

Abdominal fluttering was a sign of stress. Hmmm? That had to be it. She was under stress having all of these eyes on her.

But that still didn't account for Arthur's words. It had sounded as though he'd asked her to marry him. That couldn't be right. She had to be hearing things. Luckily, that problem was easily solved.

"I'm sorry," she said. "I think I hallucinated for a second. Could you repeat what you just said?"

Arthur cleared his throat. He took a deep breath. He also finally let her go. But not entirely.

Arthur steadied her on her feet. Then he took both her hands in his own. His hands were large and rough. Morgan's finger pads felt the calluses of his palms. One of her index fingers landed on his lifeline. It was a long and thick groove. It felt as though her index finger could fall into the groove of his life.

But then he shifted and her fingertips were held in his. His thumbs rested on the backs of her knuckles. Morgan's head tilted down to find Arthur on bended knee.

Out of the corner of her eye, she saw Percy fist pump with approval. He was the only one. A gasp swept through the entire hall, like a wave crashing out to sea instead of on land. On the faces of the ladies gathered, Morgan spied the looks of horror, of disbelief, of envy.

Morgan knew they all wanted Arthur's attention.

They all wanted to be the Lady of the Castle. And they could have at it. As soon as whatever was happening was over. She'd slip away to her room and they could get back to their revelry.

Hopefully, Arthur would be in a good mood in the morning, after he made his proposal to Lady Constance, and then Morgan could tell him of her plans with little to no issue. He'd be too busy with a wedding to prepare for and a fiancée on his arm to spare too much attention to her.

What Morgan still couldn't puzzle out was why Arthur was down on his knee? Maybe he was checking to see if she were injured? Yes, that had to be it.

But he was looking up at her. There was something in his light eyes that she'd never seen before. Something dark and warm. It felt palpable and dangerous. But she had no fear of it. Instead, she was curious.

Arthur squeezed her hand. It brought her attention back to the rest of his face. "Morgan, would you do me the honor of being my wife?"

This time Morgan's heart stopped. It tripped and skipped a beat. The irregular rhythm could be a sign of A-Fib. Atrial fibrillation was a known phenomenon when the upper and lower chambers of the heart became out of synch due to the timing of the heart's contractions which was controlled by the impulses from the heart's electrical system. But a man on his knees couldn't bring that on.

Morgan was running out of explanations. Whenever that happened, she always resorted to Occam's Razor; the idea that when presented with a number of answers to a hypothesis it was typically the simplest one that was the explanation.

A man on his knee. Looking up at a woman. Asking her to be his wife. Perhaps, just maybe, and this was a far-fetched idea, but it was statistically possible that Arthur was proposing to her.

Best to be clear.

"Me?" Morgan said. "You want me to marry you?"

"Yes," Arthur said.

"You want the two of us to partake in an ancient ritual that would legally and formally recognize that we are no longer singular individuals but a union?"

Arthur shifted on his knee but didn't get up. "Yes."

"You want to take me as your dutiful wife, who will remain under your protection, bare your children, and serve as your helpmate to run this castle?"

Now Arthur stood. But he did not let go of

Morgan's hands. He opened his mouth to speak but Morgan wasn't done with her search for clarity.

"You want to forsake all others and stay with me until death do us part?" she asked.

"Yes, Morgan. That is what I'm offering."

"If that's the case ..." She yanked her hands out of his hold. "... then the answer is absolutely, unequivocally, no."

CHAPTER ELEVEN

Arthur's grip on Morgan's forearm was ironclad. He tried to tell himself to gentle his touch, to not scare her. But what he really wanted to do was shake her.

And so his fingers dug into the flesh of her armpit. It couldn't be helped. He frogmarched Morgan out of the ballroom and into the Throne Room. It was the first time in his life that he'd manhandled a witch.

What had he been thinking asking her to marry him? And in such a public fashion. Morgan had always been ornery and unpredictable. She'd likely said no just to spite him.

The problem was she didn't have a choice. Neither of them had a choice any longer. Not now that they'd been caught in an embrace. Not once, but twice.

Arthur had strung up men for less, for daring to defile a lady under his care. And now he was the defiler. And like all the men he'd forced into matrimony, he too would do his duty. And so would she, if she knew what was good for her.

He let go of her arm the moment they crossed into the Throne Room. Then he paced away from her. His body was tense as his muscles quivered with anger.

Morgan stared at him, dark blue eyes as wide as saucers. Lips parted in a frightened O. Yet no words escaped her. She hadn't said anything since her rejection. That, her silence, unnerved Arthur the most.

He kept a fair amount of distance between them as he paced. He was unsure of himself, uncertain what he'd do to her.

He'd gotten down on his knee like some lovesick squire, for God's sake. It had to be the hart. That was the only logical explanation. The hart and its magical pheromones were affecting his judgment.

Morgan finally gathered herself to speak. "I don't know what I did to piss you off—"

"Language!"

Morgan grit her teeth. "I don't know what archaic rule I broke, or what etiquette I stepped on, but I think humiliating me in front of the whole town was a bit too far."

"Humiliate? You?" He had to take a breath between each word. Both came out in a huff that would've blown down a house of sticks.

"Yes." She held her chin high. "With that spectacle of getting down on your knee and making a show of a proposal. That was an inventive punishment, for sure."

"Punishment?" he said. He needed to stop parroting her. She had somehow frogmarched him into her crazy. "You think that was a punishment?"

"Well …" She waggled her head, as though trying to shake out any other sensible answer. "What else could it have been?"

"A proposal."

Morgan snorted. "You weren't serious."

Arthur dragged his hand over the back of his neck and through his hair.

"You know I believe courtly love is a crock of crap."

Arthur felt his Adam's apple bobbing up and down as he tried to swallow past the lump in his throat and failed.

"You can't possibly want to marry me."

Arthur stopped pacing and faced Morgan.

Morgan lowered her chin and stared at him.

The two stood before each other. Light and dark eyes roamed the other, searching for any other answer. But when Arthur's gaze met Morgan's there it was. The same answer as before.

"Perhaps this is salvageable," said a voice from far away.

Arthur turned to see Sir Bors coming up close. Behind him were Gwin and Lance. Lance shut the door so that the village onlookers wouldn't get any more drama.

"If the lady does not wish to marry," said Bors, "then we cannot force her."

All eyes went to Morgan, but she looked at Arthur, as though he were a puzzle whose edges she had long ago completed, and she was now trying to suss out the middle portion. She was likely wondering if he could force her. She'd thought he was trying to punish her? A life with him would be punishment in her eyes?

"There are other ladies who do wish for the role," Bors continued.

All eyes now swayed to Arthur. Bors was right. He could salvage this. He could marry Lady

Constance. It had been a moment of madness when he'd dropped to his knee before Morgan.

"Lady Morgan's reputation will be ruined," Arthur said. "We were seen embracing twice."

"*Pfft*," said Morgan. "I don't care about my reputation."

"I care about your reputation," said Arthur. "You're under my care."

"I don't want to be under your care. I want to go to school."

"Not this again." Arthur pinched the bridge between his nose. Then he scrubbed his fingers through his beard. "It's too dangerous— Wait. Where, exactly, did you go in Cardiff?"

"I went to Cardiff University, to the Science Department. I had an interview. Well, actually it wasn't an interview. It was more of a meet and greet because they'd already decided they want me."

"Want you?" Arthur felt something heating up his blood. He felt the urge to reach out to Morgan, to snatch her back into his embrace. He wanted to hunt down these scientists who wanted her and help them understand exactly who she belonged to. He took a step back from her and that insane urge.

"They offered me a fellowship on a research team," Morgan was saying.

And then the squeeing began. Gwin and Morgan bounced around like two school girls. Their high pitched wails assailed his ears causing him to rock back on his heels.

Arthur braced himself for a headache. But it didn't come. The smile on Morgan's face washed over him and took control of his senses again. As she shone bright, Arthur's mouth watered.

"Oh, Gwin, the campus was magical. Everyone with their heads in books. And the science department ..." Morgan paused, her eyes rolling back in her head in ecstasy.

Arthur's pants tightened. He needed to look away from her or to at least stand behind something so as to not further embarrass himself. But he couldn't move.

She was already too far away from him. He wanted to take the necessary two steps to bring her back within his reach. Then he would snake his arms around her back and pull her to him. But before he could enact that irrational idea, someone put a hand on his arm.

"Are you truly considering her for your Lady, my Lord?" asked Bors.

It was madness. Morgan could barely keep her room straight much less run a castle. That silver tongue of hers, which never edited the words of her head as they came out of her mouth, would leave diplomacy in tatters. But those hips, he knew they'd offer him a path to heaven and in return give him strong sons.

"She has no magic," Bors continued. "She's not a true witch any longer. How can she expect to run the castle?"

"Gwin is still the Lady of the Castle, so long as my brother lives," Arthur said. "The title could remain hers after, unless she remarried."

Out of the corner of his eye, Arthur saw Lance stiffen. Arthur couldn't blame his friend. What he'd said, what he was contemplating was a dick move. Couldn't be helped. That's all he was thinking with at the moment.

The two Galahad girls chattered on, ignoring the men deciding their fate.

"It's not too late," said Bors, dropping all pretense at diplomacy now. "You can still choose my daughter."

Arthur could scarcely think of ... who was his daughter again? All that filled his mind was the raven-haired witch, smiling and squeeing with delight. It was already too late. Arthur's mind was made up.

CHAPTER TWELVE

The sun greeted Morgan the next day. She'd had the weirdest dream. Atoms had flown about in her resting mind. They'd been sliced open by a sword to reveal their protons and electrons. Then fused together with things that shouldn't be unified. It had been weird.

Looking out the window, Morgan saw a rainbow appear in the distance. She wasn't the romantic sort, but she took the refracted light display as a sign. She was on the right path.

For years, she'd hidden away in this castle. But today, she was going to start showing her colors. Unlike the rainbow, she would be within reach. In fact, she'd be reaching the pot of gold.

Okay, not the best comparison. What she meant

was she was going for it. She was joining Simon Accolon's team whether Arthur liked it or not.

She fired up her computer and shot an email to Simon. A moment later his reply came back. It was done. She was now a member of the Science Department at Cardiff University. She'd start on Monday.

Yesterday had been absurd. Arthur on his knee asking her to marry him. All because of an embrace or two. Sure, they had been nice embraces. She didn't have much to compare them to. None of the knights or squires had ever offered her anything other than a pat on the back or a squeeze in greeting.

Arthur had embraced her. Held her close like she'd seen lovers do. It had been a mistake. And it was just the way of Camelot that a mistake carried with it dire consequences. Just another reason why it was absurd to ever consider her for the role as the Lady of the Castle.

Morgan pulled on a t-shirt. This one listed the chemical elements Beryllium, Nickel, and Cerium. Their elemental names spelled "Be Nice." She slipped into a peasant skirt and boots and headed out of her room.

Gwin was already up and about her business. Loren still wasn't back from her latest quest. Morgan knew her cousin would get a kick out of yesterday's events. She pulled out her cell phone to shoot off a quick text. Somehow, there was access to Wi-Fi in Asgard.

Giles and Niles Fletcher chased after each other, nearly colliding into Morgan. They pumped their feet to stop before slamming into her.

"Sorry, my lady."

"How do you do this morning, my lady?"

Morgan frowned at the two. The kids all knew she much preferred Miss Morgan to being called a lady. "What's this all about? What mischief are you up to?"

"No mischief," said Niles. "You're going to be the Lady of the Castle now."

"Mother says we need to mind ourselves around you," said Giles.

Morgan opened her mouth, but shock filled her jowls. Before she could exhale and get words out, the two brothers were off. By the time Morgan had recovered her wits, they were gone. Annora Godfrey made her way around the corner.

"Oh, Lady Morgan," Annora gushed. "I heard everything. Was it terribly romantic when Lord Arthur proposed? I heard he went down on one knee."

In Annora's hands was a bridal magazine of all things. Beneath it was a science journal. Morgan snatched the trashy mag from the top of the pile leaving behind the more appropriate intellectual one.

"I'm not marrying Arthur," she said.

"Of course you are," Annora frowned. "He asked you."

"We don't have to do things just because a man tells us to."

"But he's not a man. He's a lord. He's *our* lord."

Osbert Clarke turned the corner, coming near them. "Good morning, Lady Morgan. Congratulations on your engagement."

"I'm not engaged," Morgan huffed.

"But Arthur asked you."

"I said no," Morgan insisted. "And, besides, he didn't mean it. It was just his archaic sense of duty. Lucky for him, I'm a modern girl."

"Oh, okay," said Osbert, not sounding at all convinced. "Well, then. Oh, hello, Annora. I didn't see you there."

Annora only gulped. Without another word, Osbert took off with a friendly wave.

Once he was out of earshot, Annora gripped Morgan's forearm and whispered in desperation.

"He barely knows I'm alive. You have to tell me what you did to win Lord Arthur's attention. Was it the whole pretending to not be interested in him thing?"

"I wasn't pretending."

"But it worked. Was it the whole arguing like cats and dogs thing? I'm good at debate. But only with facts."

This was why Morgan wanted to teach science. Girls needed their heads filled with things other than courtship.

"You want to know what I did to curry Arthur's attention? I used my brain instead of following along blindly. When he said something that wasn't logical I challenged him at every turn."

"That certainly did get my attention."

Morgan grimaced not wanting to turn around and face her nemesis. Because that's what Arthur was to her; a nemesis, not a hero.

But she had to face this. This fallacy couldn't go on any longer. They needed to set the record straight.

And so Morgan turned to find the dark knight looking not at her but at Annora. He had a brilliant smile for the young lady. It caught Morgan off guard. She was so used to seeing him looking sternly at her.

Arthur bent down to be on Annora's level. "Lady

Morgan is right. A man needs a woman to challenge him every once in a while. He needs to remember that she's worth the fight."

Arthur glanced up at Morgan on that last statement. Morgan's flight or fight instincts kicked in. Her mind told her to flee this danger. But her reaction was too slow. By the time Arthur straightened, she still hadn't taken off.

"May I walk with you?" He offered his arm.

Morgan stared at the proffered limb.

"It's not a trick, Morgan."

"Why don't I believe you?"

"You know I don't lie."

No. But was he telling the whole truth? Only one way to find out; test the hypothesis.

Arthur grinned. "Are you weighing the variables out in your head?"

She frowned at him. Then she took his arm out of spite. "Are you going to try to change my mind about marriage?"

"Yes. But not right now. I wanted to know more about your research. You said you were offered a -a fellowship was it? For nuclear science, if I heard you and Gwin correctly? I thought your field was chemistry."

"It is. It was. I've dabbled in chemistry, physics, and biology."

"Dabbled? I would've expected you to say you mastered them."

They turned a corner and came to a small crowd of townsfolk. Mostly women. The others pretended not to stare, but no one ever said a witch was a good actress. They looked away too quickly and whispered just a touch too loudly.

Morgan hated gossip. When it was about her. She could talk smack about others for days on end, so long as her name was left out of it.

"What are these human scientists interested in?" Arthur asked as he led her outside.

"They're trying to add to the Periodic Table of Elements. They're on the path to discovering a new element. The Periodic Table is—"

"I know what the Periodic Table is, Morgan. The known list of natural and synthesized elements all organized by atomic number."

"They're close to finding more, and I think I know a way to help them."

"Would these be nuclear elements?"

Ah. Now she saw the trajectory of this conversation. "Don't let the term nuclear put you off.

Those elements have been used to power whole cities and help fight against cancer."

Morgan lifted her gaze, expecting Arthur to be gazing down upon her with skepticism. But his gaze was thoughtful. Interested. A small smile played at the corner of his lip.

"I never get to see this side of you," he said. "The passionate side."

"Because you're not interested in science."

"That's not true. Math was my best subject in university even though I was a history major."

Morgan knew Arthur's degree was in Military History. But she hadn't known that bit about math. "You took math beyond the required freshman math?"

"I gained enough credits for it to be a second Minor."

"You actually studied math?"

Arthur laughed. When he did, that small grin split wider. But it was lopsided. The side closest to her opened wide and Morgan felt the sensation that he might eat her up. And still, she didn't run.

"I studied calculus," he said. "Before you were born. I've just never had a cause to use it here."

"Calculus is around us every day. It's used in web

searches on the internet. Meteorologists use it in weather forecasts. You see it in architecture. It stops the spread of some infectious diseases. I could go on."

Arthur waited patiently, as though he'd actually like her to go on. He'd usually stop her talking by now. His eyes would darken; his mouth would set in a firm line of disapproval. But his gray eyes were soft now. His lips pulled back in that small, lopsided grin.

"Did you know your eyes light up when you talk about science?" he said. "Like a blue fire."

"Blue is the hottest part of the flame."

Arthur stared deeply into her eyes. Morgan felt her entire face heat, as though his eyes were a flame and its rays were touching her cheeks.

"I've never considered putting your talents to use," he said. "I apologize for that. You must've felt useless all these years."

"I ... I ..." She had no words. She had no idea what was happening here. All logic and processes failed her.

"I'll do better," he said. He'd stopped walking. He faced her and held her hands, the same way he'd done last night. Morgan looked from his hands to his eyes, and then down at his knees.

Was he going to get down on his knee again and propose? Did she want him to?

He didn't bend the knee. He rubbed the rough pads of his fingers over the backs of her knuckles. It was surprisingly soothing.

"I'm not going to ask you that question again," he said, as though he were reading her mind.

"Oh?" Morgan felt the disappointment crash in the pit of her stomach.

"Not until I earn it."

"Earn it? You mean like in some courtly love quest where you go on crazy impossible challenges to prove your devotion?"

"I was going to do this the hard way and ask you on a date. But if you want a quest, I'd prefer that challenge. Those are easy."

He was serious. He wasn't taking it back. He was going to go forward with this idea that they should be married.

"You don't have to do this," she said. "We could just tell everyone it was a mistake and they'll believe us."

Arthur shrugged, but he didn't disagree.

"We both know I'd make you a terrible wife," she continued. "Constance would make a far better lady."

Arthur nodded, but he still didn't let go of her hand.

"This doesn't make any sense, Arthur. Why me?"

He shrugged his shoulders again, then waggled his head, and finally, his brows lifted to his hairline.

"I don't know?" he said. "But the hypothesis is in my head. I figured we could do the experiment together. Test the variables and see what we come up with."

Morgan's breath caught at the scientific proposal. She felt the synapses in her brain firing to get started on the trial. He was still holding onto her hands, only lightly. Morgan's fingers curled around his.

CHAPTER THIRTEEN

"Maybe you hit your head yesterday during training? Or while out hunting?"

Arthur tried and failed to hide his smile at Morgan's latest query. For the past quarter of an hour, she'd tried to explain away his sudden interest in her. She'd considered he'd eaten mushrooms and was hallucinating. She'd outright asked if he was on human drugs. Or just plain drunk.

Arthur wasn't seeing or hearing things that weren't there. Neither had he taken any medication; prescribed, illegal, or magical. He had all of his senses and wits about him as he walked with Morgan's hand tucked into the crook of his arm.

Each time she presented a new theory, she

squeezed his bicep with excitement. She'd tilt her face up, blue eyes blazing bright as a bulb lit with an idea. That shine dimmed the insult of her accusations against his misdiagnosed insanity and imaginary drug use.

Morgan felt right on Arthur's arm. The brush of her body against his side sent thrills coursing through his blood. He wanted to tighten his grip on her, to turn her to him, and taste the next preposterous premise that parted her lips.

He no longer cared why he felt this way. This way of being was his new reality. Morgan, by his side, cradled in the crook of his body, was his future.

Coming back to the present, Arthur laughed at her next conjecture. She'd gone so far in search of an answer that now she pondered if he was experiencing a past life regression.

"Morgan La Faye and King Arthur were enemies in the lore," she said. "And everyone in Camelot knows there's an element of truth in each of those stories."

"Morgan, we knew these people. If not directly, then we know the truth of their lives. There was no incest in my family history. Nor was there any infidelity. All of my male ancestors were devoted to their wives."

"Because they were in love."

Arthur nodded.

"But you don't love me."

"I like you."

"No, you don't." The chiding smile on Morgan's face sweetened the sting of her words.

"Well," he conceded, "you *have* been a pain."

"Well," she huffed, "you *have* been a fascist."

Morgan tugged away from him, but he wouldn't let go. He settled his free hand over hers and rubbed the rough skin over her knuckles.

"I'll say this," he said. "You've certainly kept me on my toes."

They stood in a grove not too far from the castle grounds. A few of the hart's blooms poked up through the loosening earth. Their golden stamen eyes twinkling at them as though they approved this pairing.

From the flowers poking out of the ground, Arthur's gaze roamed from Morgan's booted feet that had to take two steps in order to keep pace with his. His eyes trailed up to the peak of flesh between the top of her boots and just above her knee. The skirt she wore was the weakest chainmail, made of cotton instead of metal. He'd need no sword to penetrate that thin layer of protection.

He had to swallow before continuing up over curves that rivaled the sharp bend of a scythe. His gaze lingered on the mounds on her chest. The twin spikes that pushed at the fabric caused his vision to flail.

Morgan crossed her arms over her chest and looked away from him, her face flaming. "When you look at me like that I don't know what to do."

Arthur had to remember that she was untried, unpracticed. He'd have to take his time with her. There were so many reasons she would scare.

The notion that they didn't belong together.

The notion that someone else was more suited for him than her.

The notion that she was a woman of intelligence who wanted to leave the confines of this town and explore the academic world.

The notion that she was a lady untouched and unwise to the base desires of a man.

"I'm sorry." Arthur's voice croaked.

He balled his hands at his sides to keep them to himself. But he continued to invade her space nonetheless. He wracked his brain for the words to make her comfortable, to set her at ease.

Morgan rounded on him. Her hands thrown up

in frustration. "So, this isn't a bet between you and Percy?"

"A ... what?"

"Like in one of those bad teen movies where the popular guy makes a bet with his douchey friend that he can make over the ugly, friendless, nerdy girl into the beautiful, popular prom queen."

Arthur didn't watch a lot of movies. Not the action movies where play actors blew things up and left a trail of bodies. He'd seen enough real-life action in his days to be entertained by the sets and props.

He didn't care for the romantic comedies either. He found them wholly unrealistic. Especially at the end with the fault always lying with the man who would then have to make an over the top gesture at the end of the film over a misunderstanding that could've been avoided if the woman had only talked to him.

And forget about teen movies. He hadn't been a teenager in two hundred years. Needless to say, he couldn't relate to whatever it was Morgan was trying to say to him.

"You think my courtship of you is based on a dare?" he asked.

Morgan hesitated, still avoiding his gaze. Arthur

didn't like the way she was closed off to him. He unballed his fists and reached out one hand to her. He tugged at the fingertips of one of her hands until they uncurled from her forearm. Then he went and worked on the other hand.

Morgan chanced a look at him. Her gaze shaded and vulnerable. He wanted to press a kiss to her eyelids, to press his certainty into her. But he held onto his patience and pressed their palms together instead.

"It just defies the laws of physics," she said.

"Really? Name one infraction?"

"Newton's First Law of Motion. It states that a body at rest remains at rest, while a body in motion stays in motion."

"I know this one." Words rolled off his tongue, but all of his focus was on the fleshy part of her palm. He had the strongest urge to bite it. "The law of constants."

"Yes, exactly."

"How did we break that?"

"The other part of the law has to do with force," she said. "A constant velocity is only stopped by an unbalanced force."

Arthur nodded as he tried to follow along with her logic. But he was more interested in the way her lips constantly moved in the formation of words. He was feeling rather off balance himself.

"I was minding my own business," Morgan said. "Moving at a constant speed nowhere near you. Yet here you are and my world has stopped."

Yes. That was exactly how he felt. Like there was a sudden crash and, when he found his way out, she was standing there. Right in front of him. Blocking his way. Just like she was now.

Her blue eyes gazed up at him; open, clear. But there was a crinkle at the edges. "Where did the force come from?" she asked.

"Neither of us *believe* in magic, Morgan. We know magic to be real. Even though others can't see it."

He took another step closer to her. He wanted to eliminate the distance entirely. But he knew better. He had to move slowly upon his prey before he could snare her.

"There's something here." Arthur indicated the open space between them, still holding both her hands in his. "I think you feel it too."

She didn't answer. Her eyes searched his, moving rapidly as though reading a book she didn't understand, but still wouldn't put down.

Keeping her hand in his, Arthur ran a fingertip

over her brow. Her lids hooded with his motion, and he felt sorry for the loss of her full blue gaze.

"You think me capable of such a cruel joke?" he asked.

"Well ..." She bit the inside of her lip and looked down.

It was a good thing she looked down. Otherwise, she would've seen the desire flare in Arthur's eyes. He felt his face flame, his body tighten with want. Had this been a true hunt, he'd have already released his bow and taken a shot. Holding still and laying in wait for Morgan was the hardest thing he'd ever had to do.

"Maybe not you," she said, "with your overdose of chivalry. But Percy?"

"He wouldn't ..." But Arthur's voice trailed off as he gave it more thought.

Morgan raised a doubtful brow. Her blue eyes filled with mirth. A small smile tugged at her lips.

"With a human maybe," Arthur conceded. "But not with a witch."

"If he even considered it on me, I'd go total Carrie on his ass. Pigs' blood over the gaming room door."

Arthur chuckled. She was a firebrand. Funny; that same thought used to irk him. Now, it delighted him. There would be no monotony with her by his side. Every day would be an adventure. But that was enough for today.

"Hush now," he growled low. "Watch your language."

"You're not the boss of me." But there was a tremor in her defiance.

"Be a good girl," he chided.

Morgan inhaled sharply at his command. Before she could come up with a retort, Arthur pressed his lips to her forehead. There was a deep crease there at the first touch of his lips. But as he lingered a second longer than prudent, he felt the crease lines loosen, and then disappear completely.

Her nose rested just beneath his chin and he felt her nostrils flare. Her lips were aimed at the column of his neck and he felt the heat of her exhale. He looked down at her. She looked up at him.

He could do it. He could take her right now, at this moment. The entire town already believed them to be engaged. He'd be breaking no rule. He'd overstep no boundary.

Arthur stepped away from her and offered her his arm. Morgan stared at the proffered appendage. Confusion evident on her beautiful face.

"I've taken enough of your time," he said. "Let's get you back to the castle before you're missed."

Arthur only felt a slight pang of remorse when she heeded his command. Instead, he felt a surge of joy that she'd listened to him. She walked with him, taking more of the necessary steps to enact his plan. Everyone else might have accepted the engagement, but the most important person still wasn't convinced.

Arthur promised himself that he wouldn't take that first kiss until his intended came to the realization, the undeniable belief, the irrefutable truth, the magical actuality, that she was meant to be his.

At some point in her second decade of life, Morgan's mother had bound her with a tutu, strapped her into soft, pink slippers, and deposited her in the town's only dance class. The other girls twirled around and leaped past Morgan who could never keep the beat.

Sure, she could do the dance moves when called to the center of Madame Guillaume's class to demonstrate. Her pirouettes were perfect. Her *jettes* were grand. But once the music started, Morgan was all over the place and nowhere near where she should be in the dance line or on the beat.

Beat deafness it was called. It afflicted a small, minuscule portion of the planet's population, but it was real. Its victims were people who couldn't catch a beat, clap to a rhythm, or move in synch.

Every living creature had a natural internal rhythm. Their heart beat at a steady clip. They walked or slithered or swam to a particular pace. There was even a particular gait at which animals made vocal or sonar communications.

This internal measure came from an oscillating wave somewhere deep within the body. Unless you were beat deaf. For the rhythmically challenged, that same internal oscillator had a different frequency.

Meaning Morgan had truly marched to the beat of her own drum for her entire life.

When Arthur had pulled her near, she'd felt in tune with something outside of herself for the first time in her life. It was dizzying. And now that she walked on her own, her internal rhythm was off.

This would not do.

She was an autonomous child of God. She had not given her sovereignty for a man to lord over her. Although, she had allowed Arthur to take liberties with her body that no man had ever inquired about.

The thought of that kiss on her forehead sent her reeling. Now inside the castle, she reached out for the wall but met with a shelf. Bumping into the shelf made it oscillate and a vase shook, scooting to the edge.

It was an expensive vase from the 12th century. The vase teetered just at the edge of Morgan's grasp. Morgan opened her palm to call it back, but no magic pulsed out of her hand. The vase sailed to the ground, preparing to shatter into tiny, depreciated fragments. But at the last second, it hovered in the air.

An inch above the ground, the vase's downward trajectory stopped. Morgan's palm was still open. Warmth pulsed at the center of her hand. Her gut burned with an unsaturated desire.

Could it be? Had her magic come back? Igraine had said it was possible, that the Spear of Destiny's blade may not have taken every last drop of her powers from her.

"I've got it," said a voice from behind her.

Morgan shut her eyes, extinguishing that feeble ember of hope. She balled her fist, her fingers cold as they met her palm. As the vase retook its place on the mantel, Morgan fixed her features carefully before turning to face Constance.

Once she was certain the vase was secure, Constance lowered her magic-filled palms and met

Morgan's gaze. "Congratulations on your engagement, Lady Morgan."

Morgan's forehead wrinkled as she studied the other woman. Those wrinkles had a hard time finding their groove. One reason was that Morgan still felt the lingering pressure of Arthur's kiss there. The other reason was that Constance spoke without any malice. Constance's own brow furrowed with disappointment. But her smile, though not as bright as usual, was honest.

"I don't know how all this happened." Morgan lifted her hollow palms skyward, as though their emptiness were evidence. "It wasn't my intention. Just yesterday, I couldn't stand the man. And now ..."

Morgan let the sentence trail off. But she watched its trajectory with interest. Because she had no idea where this thing between her and Arthur was going.

"I must admit I was surprised," Constance was saying. "And I am disappointed for myself. But I am happy he'll be with the woman he loves."

Love? No. That's not what was happening here. Morgan backed up, her hands in front of her brushing away the idea.

"Oh, no," she said. "He doesn't love me. It's just ... You see ..."

But how could Morgan explain something she didn't understand herself?

She couldn't deny that there was a thing between the two of them. All she wanted to do was go to her lab, pull out her books and measuring tools, and examine this thing from every angle until she understood what, exactly, was happening.

"I've seen the way he looks at you," said Constance.

"The way he looks at me?" Morgan parroted.

"I just never thought you were interested."

"I wasn't." Not before. But now …?

"You've always been so independent and against much of what the Knight's Code of Chivalry entails." Constance gave Morgan a chiding smile that lacked any sting.

Even though there was no bite to the other woman's words, Morgan's hackles went up. "Just because I'm a feminist doesn't mean I hate men. And just because I don't want to be coddled doesn't mean I don't want to be treated like a lady."

As Morgan's voice rose, Constance's smile faltered.

Morgan shut her eyes and took a deep breath. She placed her index finger behind her ears and massaged, hoping to regain her equilibrium.

"I'm sorry, Constance. I'm just a bit off balance today."

"It's understandable." Constance's voice was polite, but that politeness was now at a distance.

"Would you excuse me? I think I'm going to go to my room and lie down."

"Of course."

Constance nodded and stepped out of Morgan's way. But down the hall, Morgan saw other ladies lying in wait for her. None wore the sincere smile that Constance had shone her. Fake happiness coated their faces like the icing on a cake left out overnight; hard, flaky, and lacking its original sweetness.

Luckily, her sister was an angel of mercy.

"Morgan," Gwin called from the stair in the Great Hall. "You have an urgent phone call. You can take it in my office."

Morgan rushed past the receiving line of women who had been in competition for Arthur's hand. She tried to hold her head high and regal as she walked the line. But her ears twitched as she caught unflattering whispers. Her nose itched as she smelled green envy. Her molars ground as she held her tongue instead of lashing out at the busybody naysayers.

When she made it to the stair, Gwin looped Morgan's arm through hers and ushered her up the stairs. And by ushered, Gwin yanked Morgan up the planks and shoved her sister inside the office.

"Gwin—"

Gwin continued her yanking and shoving, closing the office door and pushing Morgan down into the seat behind her desk.

"Lucy, you got some 'splaining to do!"

Morgan turned her confused expression from her sister to the open laptop. Another blonde haired woman filled the screen. Blue eyes peered at Morgan, glossy red lips twisted.

"Hey, cuz," Morgan sighed.

"Don't you 'hey cuz' me," said Loren. "You and Arthur?"

"You said this was an emergency." Morgan glared at Gwin.

"You went and got yourself engaged to Arthur," said Gwin. "This called for an emergency Galahad girl meeting."

"I can't believe you finally snagged him," said Loren.

"I did not snag anything," said Morgan. "And what do you mean *finally*?"

"She fell into his arms after sneaking around

with him at the ball." Gwin bent her head down so that her face was within the frame.

"We weren't sneaking," said Morgan. "Well, I was sneaking, but not with him. And I haven't said yes."

"And you don't have to agree to anything," said another voice. Dr. Nia Rivers poked her brown head onto the screen, blocking the view of Loren.

Finally. Someone who spoke some sense. Someone who didn't immediately assume that Morgan's inevitable path ended on Arthur's arm.

"Forced marriage is akin to slavery and it's illegal in all of the United Kingdom," said Nia. "I'm not one to bring humans and their laws into the magical world, but I will if I have to."

"He's not forcing me," Morgan tried, but no one was listening. Once again she was marching to one beat while everyone else sang a different tune.

"See, I told you." Loren gave her best friend a shove so that she dominated the screen once more. "I saw this coming. All that hidden passion, all that arguing."

"There was no hidden passion," said Morgan.

"I believe you, Morgan," said Nia. "Arthur has no hidden depths."

Morgan scrunched her nose, no longer willing to

go that far. Arthur had shown her a different side of himself today; an academic side. Morgan had found that depth worth investigating.

"He got down on one knee when he asked her," said Gwin.

"No way," said Loren.

"Did you kick him?" asked Nia. Her pretty features scrunched in confusion. "Or punch him in the gut? He'll crumple like a toy soldier if you go for the knee."

Arthur and Nia had a complicated past. She liked to dig up the past and share it with the world. Arthur liked to keep his world hidden and humans at arm's length. Camelot was filled with novelties and treasures that Nia itched to expose. Needless to say, the two didn't see eye to eye. Well, that wasn't really so complicated to explain.

"It was a proposal, Nia," said Loren. "Not a fight. Getting down on one knee is what men do when they propose marriage to a woman."

"What would you know about it, Ms. Commitment Phobe?" Nia asked.

"Apparently more than the immortal who's been with the same man for hundreds of years. Yet, she won't let him put a ring on it."

Nia straightened. Only her breasts were visible on the screen, but her tone was glaringly vivid. "Are we really going there?"

Both Morgan and Gwin leaned away from the laptop. They knew better than to interject when Nia and Loren got into it. The two best friends bickered as hard and fiercely as they protected each other. But it looked like this would be a short-lived tiff since both ladies had gone for the jugular.

"We're not engaged right now," Morgan said. "Not exactly."

Gwin peered down at her. Loren leaned into the screen. Nia bent down, face beside her bestie.

"He said he wasn't going to ask me again," said Morgan.

Gwin's eyes widened and her mouth formed a crestfallen O. Loren's gaze narrowed and she sucked in her lips making an angry sound. Nia shut her eyes and let out a relieved sigh.

"He said he'd only ask me again after he'd earned the right. He's courting me." Morgan gave a shaky laugh. "Isn't that ridiculous?"

Gwin's shoulders caved inward as she let out an *ahhh.* Loren's back straightened as she let out an *ooooh?* Nia crossed her arms over her chest as she let out a confused *hmmm?*

"So, a chaste courtship?" said Loren, her typical sarcastic, deadpan tone. "That sounds like fun."

Out of these three women, Morgan was the one with the least experience. Gwin was married. Nia was in a long-term relationship. And Loren ... well, Loren got her kicks when and wherever she could get them.

But Morgan was no longer at a zero sum. "He did kiss me—sorta."

"Sorta?" asked Loren. "If it was sorta, it wasn't a kiss, babe."

"It was on the forehead."

They all groaned in three different notes that harmonized into a chord of sadness, compassion, and pity.

"It wasn't entirely chaste," said Morgan. "He leaned into me and pressed his lips against my head. It was kinda hot. His lips, I mean. It was like he wanted more but he held himself back. At least that's what it felt like to me."

They groaned again. But the tone was decidedly different. It was breathy, and buoyant, and dreamy.

"Wow," said Nia. "He really is into you. I never would've believed Arthur capable."

"But you just said he wasn't because the kiss was chaste," said Morgan.

"That wasn't chaste, Mo," said Loren. "He's holding back. Men only hold back for the woman they want to hold on to."

Nia nodded as she rested her chin in her hand, her brown eyes took on a faraway gaze. Gwin smiled too. She twisted the band on her finger but her gaze was trained out the window which overlooked the knight's training ground.

Morgan wasn't sure what to think or feel. Did she want to be held onto? She had liked being in Arthur's arms.

"I guess Camelot will have a new Lady of the Castle," said Loren.

That brought Gwin's attention back into the room. She blinked a couple of times as though a realization was dawning.

"I thought the Lady of the Castle had to be a witch," said Nia. "Isn't there some kind of charm that protects the town through the bond of a Pendragon and a witch?"

Now, Gwin shifted on the armchair. On the screen, Loren gave Nia a punch in the boob. Morgan knew it didn't hurt. Nia was an ancient being born of a purer form of the essence running through every witch and wizard's veins. But the boob punch did its job of reminding the immortal of her manners.

"Oh, I'm sorry, Morgan. I didn't mean …" Nia let the words trail off.

No one ever knew what words to say to Morgan about the loss of her powers.

"Gwin's still the Lady of the Castle," said Morgan. "And will remain so as the wife or the widow of the eldest Pendragon."

Now Gwin balled her hands in her lap. Her gaze remained trained on her fists. Her lips quivered ever so slightly as she tried to arrange her mouth into her perpetual hostess-smile.

"Nothing's changed," said Morgan. "Right now, everything is as exactly as it was yesterday."

Gwin met her sister's gaze. "I want you to be happy."

"I want *you* to be happy," said Morgan. "And I didn't say I was going to marry him. I only agreed to a date."

The three women nodded. But Morgan could see that all of their eyes sparkled.

"You're going to make such a beautiful bride," said Loren.

"I know you qualify for white," said Nia. "But cream would go so well with your skin tone."

"You are so right about that," said Gwin.

It was like a record constantly scratching with

these three as they bounced from wedding gowns, to DJs versus bands, then flowers. Until finally they began a conversation about veils that Morgan conveniently tuned out of.

rthur's boots pounded the earth. His instep crunched fallen tree limbs in his haste. His heel snapped rocks as he ate up the distance. Yet somehow, even with his blind, forceful strides, Arthur managed to skirt the delicate blooms popping up here and there on the forest floor.

He pushed himself faster, harder. He needed the physical beating of the hard ground punishing his legs to regain mastery of his own body. He needed the wind to slap sense into his mind. He needed to push the chambers of his heart past the breaking point to cause an arrest. Then maybe it would slow down for a moment.

It didn't work. His legs wanted to race back to

her. Blue eyes clouded his mind's eye. His heartbeat tripped over itself at the very thought of her.

Morgan consumed his every waking thought. Last night she'd stolen into his dreams. He'd lost a war he didn't have a conscious memory of declaring.

Was this love? He didn't know? He'd only ever loved his parents. He knew this emotion for Morgan, this tightening that happened in his chest at the same time that it tightened his groin, was not familial love.

Neither was it mere lust. Arthur had had his fair share of women over the decades. They were all faceless and nameless now. It was only Morgan's inquisitive expression that he saw clearly.

Arthur was determined that he and Morgan would have something different in their life together. If not some great love affair, then at least a relationship that challenged them both and was filled with passion and humor. That was something to build on.

Once she agreed to marry him.

He wasn't too worried about her acceptance. The proposal had been a shock to her, a shock to all of them. However, it appeared she was processing it now. He just had to keep her analytical mind engaged like he had on their walk yesterday.

Morgan's eyes had lit up when he'd compared their courtship to a science experiment. Her excitement hadn't dwindled as they'd returned to the castle without having drawn a conclusion. She seemed eager to find another way to approach the study of the thing between them.

Morgan wasn't one for romance. This would be a methodical process, like a well thought out battle plan. That line of thinking excited Arthur.

How would he approach her next? What tactic would he use to corner her? What would be the best method to breach her defenses and get those walls down.

Behind him, he heard the sound of horse hooves racing to reach his pace. The magical steeds of Camelot could easily reach seventy miles per hour. In today's hunt, they had nothing on Arthur.

He was done with this cat and mouse game with the hart. Done with this gentleman's game of manners and protocol. Done chasing after what would inevitably be his. The hart would be his today. And soon after, all of the perks that came with ending this game would be his spoils.

Morgan had seen him off this morning. There had been no words exchanged between them. They hadn't even touched. She'd stood in the door of the castle next to her sister as Gwin sent the men off with strong coffee, protein-rich snacks, and words of encouragement.

Morgan had leaned against the door frame. Her gaze had rested boldly upon him. She'd regarded Arthur as though he were a troubling mathematical problem and she was trying to do the sums in her head. It didn't look like she was getting anywhere.

As the mists rose above the mote, Arthur had smiled at Morgan's mystified expression. His grin must have startled her. Her blue eyes refocused and then her gaze darted about. Arthur held still until she resettled on him.

She gave a little shrug of her shoulder as though to say *Fine, you caught me.* Then her brow quirked up in that defiant way he'd once found annoying. *What are you going to do about it?* that gaze asked. Arthur's smile broadened, and he let out a silent chuckle.

She was funny. He'd known she was funny. He'd just never had leave to laugh at any of her biting wit because it was usually his ass her jokes chomped down on. But now that he was included in the joke, now that he stood in the light of her smile, he was happy to sit in the audience.

In answer to her question, he knew exactly what he was going to do about it. He was going to shoot an arrow through a proud animal's heart and force it to yield.

The animal in question raced into view. The hart reached a speed beyond the supernatural. Arthur kept pace with it, quickly closing in.

The beast was nearly within the boundaries of Arthur's crosshairs. Arthur just needed to get a few paces closer. But he was already pushing past his top speed.

Something inside him gave him a kick that turbocharged his legs and made him sprint even harder. The hart was within range. Man and beast ran for the lives they wanted, both of their days numbered.

The hart didn't slow its speed. It kept moving forward, barreling toward the side of a small hillside. Even if it had escaped a pointed end, it would still be cornered.

Arthur lifted his bow. It was insane to take a shot at a running target. Homicidal to take that same shot while running himself. Wayward, misjudged, and misplaced arrows always caused more harm than good. But it was just Arthur and the hart. No one else was near.

Arthur released the shot. The power of the release sent a shockwave through his fingertips that made his whole body clench. His breath caught as he watched the quiver sail across the air. He didn't dare blink, because in a blink, his whole life would change.

Standing in the sunlight, the snow melting around him as he waited for death to present itself, Arthur held his eyes wide.

The glow of Morgan's smile was still on his mind. He eagerly anticipated the time when he could taste those lips. It still baffled him that Morgan, of all people, would have him feeling like a giddy teenager.

But here he was, daydreaming about those curves, those eyes, those lips. Very soon those bow-shaped lips would be meeting his. He just had to be sure and duck out of the way of that second arrow.

Second arrow?

A second arrow whizzed just over the head of the stampeding hart. It nicked Arthur's arrowhead, sending its trajectory askew by mere inches, and missing the hart. Both shafts fell with an impotent clatter to the cold, hard ground as the hart raced on.

Arthur lifted his head. Standing a mere thirty feet away was Lance. His red hair was a flame in the snow-covered forest. His light-colored eyes burned into Arthur.

"What the hell?" growled Arthur.

"Oh?" Lance placed his hand on his chest. "Did I make you miss your shot? My bad."

Lance elongated the A in bad. His Scottish brogue making an appearance. Typically, Lance kept his Highland roots at bay. That accent only made an appearance when he was pissed.

"I had the hart in my sight." Arthur marched down into the glade to retrieve his arrow. He picked up Lance's and shook it at the other knight as he approached. "The beast would've been caught. Things could finally settle down."

"You mean *you* could settle down."

"Yes," said Arthur, entirely uncertain why they were shouting at each other. "Exactly."

"With Morgan."

Arthur nodded, lifting his hands up in a gesture that punctuated Lance's obvious statement.

"Morgan; a witch with no magic."

"I don't care about that."

Lance threw up his hands. "That's your problem. You think about everyone's safety, but do you at all consider their happiness?"

"What the hell are you talking about?"

"If you marry Morgan, the two of you can't establish a new covenant to protect Camelot."

The covenant between the Pendragon heir and a witch? That's what this was about? The covenant was more tradition than practical. The knights had protected Camelot and its witches for over a millennium.

"That's nothing to worry about," Arthur said. "Besides, the old covenant will stay in place. Even after my brother's death, it will still hold true as Gwin's solemn vow."

Lance's cheeks turned as red as his hair. He let out a string of curses in Gaelic. The only word Arthur caught was Gwin.

Gwin? Oh. Right. Gwin.

"She was finally going to be free," Lance growled.

Arthur's marriage would've established a new bond and a new covenant. But with Morgan being a disabled witch, that left the covenant made by Gwin and Merlin in place. Unless Gwin took vows with another man after Merlin's death. Which she would never do if she thought it would leave the people she loved unprotected.

"I know he's your brother," said Lance. "I know I'm an illegitimate bastard. But he's an actual murdering bastard."

Arthur's jaw tensed at the truthful words. He and his brother had never been close, but Merlin was still family. And you didn't turn your back on family.

"Hasn't she given enough to this place? Haven't we both? And you, you selfish bastard, you keep asking more of us."

Now Arthur saw a shade of red. "She had the chance to choose you, Lancelot. She didn't."

The silence was stony. Lance didn't like to discuss his feelings about Gwin, at least not with Arthur. Likely because he didn't want to put Arthur in the awkward position of having his best friend lusting over his brother's wife. Lance was thoughtful like that. But Arthur knew the man had been hurting for years, decades.

Lance had never had a serious relationship. Hell, the man had never had a relationship. Arthur knew he was often propositioned by the widows of the town. But the two men didn't discuss that either.

Women were an afterthought for the ginger-haired knight. It wasn't so much that they never stayed around. Rather, it was Lance who never stayed. He was always the first to volunteer for a quest, the impossible ones, the ones that should've killed him but for his stubbornness to die, and perhaps his chivalrous desire to impress a certain lady whose love he could never have.

Morgan was right. Courtly love was a crock of crap. Again, Arthur found his lips splitting into a grin at the mere thought of her. But that grin soon faded as the sound of hooves tore apart the tense silence between him and Lance.

A white blur filled Arthur's vision. The hart stampeded toward them. Having reached the boundary that was the hillside before them, the beast had turned around. It would crush them both if they didn't do something. They had only seconds to move. Unfortunately, there was another problem.

Lance had cocked back his arm, preparing to take a shot at Arthur. Arthur could dive out of the way, but that would leave Lance caught unawares. If Arthur ducked the blow, he'd escape but he'd leave Lance exposed to the hart's attack. There was only one option.

Arthur called upon all his strength to shove Lance aside. It was a difficult maneuver as he had to also duck the strong man's blow. But it worked.

Lance went tumbling to the side in a furious bundle of limbs. Arthur had just enough time to straighten and take on the hart's bulk. His resting body met with an object in constant motion. By the law of Newton, his inertia was forced into a different state.

Arthur's feet left the ground as he was swung up on the hart's rack like a coat flung on a peg near the door. The hart gave a shake of his head which sent Arthur sailing into the air. His body hit the ground with a thump and a crack. A pool of red crimson stained the melting white snow.

CHAPTER SIXTEEN

"Is it the money? Because I'm sure I can find a grant."

Morgan pressed the receiver to her ear as Simon Accolon spoke. "It's not the money," she said. "I'd do it for free."

Simon chuckled on the other end. "Never say that. Women are still paid less than their value all across the world. You'll take the whole gender back a step in the progress of the Women's Movement. Why are you stepping back now, might I ask?"

Why indeed? Morgan could hardly bring herself to say it out loud. *Because this guy who never showed interest in me is suddenly giving me the full courtly press and I kinda like it. Honestly, I really like it.*

Morgan had never walked arm and arm with a man, other than her father of course. The memory of the heat radiating off of Arthur's thick bicep, the burn of his gaze when he'd looked down at her, the blaze of warmth from his breath hitting her cheek as he'd chuckled at something she said, just thinking about it made her feel feverish.

Morgan had marveled. Half in a trance at her reactions to him. The other half of her was all data nerd as she cataloged all the stats of the encounter.

She'd been perspiring on her forehead. Her palm—where she'd held onto Arthur's bicep as they promenaded around the castle grounds—had been both damp at the center and warm at her fingertips. Her knees wobbled every few steps and she'd had to lean into him once or twice. Her pulse had raced the entire time, and her neck had been hot.

All of those symptoms pointed to a severe case of the flu. Which made sense. She had to be sick in the head to even consider this.

A courtship?

With Arthur?

She had lost all her good sense. Her thoughts whirled around in her mind like a star slipping out of orbit. Gravity eluded her because she couldn't tell which way was up from down.

Was this reality? Arthur making a play for her hand? Or could this be a ploy to get her to give up her academic pursuits and stay at home?

Morgan still wasn't sure. She still couldn't truly believe that Arthur desired her out of anything other than a sense of duty because they'd been caught in a compromising position. Twice.

Still, she'd liked having his full attention. She'd liked walking by his side. She wanted to do it again. Just to gather more data.

Meanwhile, while she was collecting input on whatever this thing was between her and Arthur, she couldn't take on the research position with Simon. But she couldn't tell him her true hesitation. She didn't want to lose his respect. So she told a modified truth.

"I have some family obligations that I need to take care of."

And, boy, would this be an obligation if she accepted it. Marriage was a life sentence. And lives were long where she came from. There was no such thing as divorce in Camelot. Death was the only way out, as her sister knew.

"I'm so sorry," said Simon. "Is someone ill?"

"Oh, no. It's nothing like that." Well, it kinda was something like that if she pointed the finger at herself. This thing had definitely afflicted her with something out of her ordinary stasis.

"Is it that your family disapproves of your scientific endeavors?" Simon asked.

"They're trying," Morgan said. It wasn't a lie. Some of them had tried.

Gwin, their father, and Igraine had always encouraged Morgan. It was her mother that had turned up her aquiline nose at Morgan's little hobby.

Arthur, too, had regarded her work with open contempt. But not yesterday. Yesterday, he'd been interested.

"I understand," said Simon.

His tone was soft, filled with concern and compassion. Morgan also detected a note of empathy. Had Simon's own family disapproved of his scientific endeavors?

"It's just that science isn't practiced in my community's ... religion," Morgan said by way of explanation.

"I can understand that, too. My parents come from different religions. My father was a devout Christian. My mother dabbled in the occult."

"The occult? What? Like a Wiccan?"

Wiccans were not admired in Camelot. They

were a nuisance that liked to dance around a fire bare-breasted. They didn't cause any harm, but the knights kept them away from any sacred place with a marked amount of ley energy.

With or without magic, a collective of like-minded women could move mountains. Literally. The Banduri had proven that time and time again. Monuments like Stonehenge were case in point.

Much of humanity thought the arrangement of stones was either a marvel of man's engineering or alien interference. It was the work of the original Banduri priestesses. And the stones weren't meant to tell time or serve as a gathering place. It was protection, their only weapon against knights and witches.

The stones of Stonehenge and other stone circle arrays around the world were made of mainly sarsen stones. The stones were, as Loren put it, witch kryptonite. A single rock could bring a knight, witch, or wizard to their knees.

"My mother's wife is a Wiccan," Simon said. "My birth mother was raised in an old, ancient religion. More cultural than spiritual. The custody battle between my parents was grueling. It nearly tore me apart."

"Are they cordial now?" Morgan asked.

"My mother's remarried and living in a commune in New Zealand. My father ... was lost to us some time ago."

"I'm so sorry for your loss."

"Oh, he's not dead. Just lost. Doesn't want to be found is more like it. He still reaches out to me from time to time. He's ... eccentric."

A sad fog settled over the communication line between them. Morgan wasn't sure how to lighten the mood. She still had both her parents. At over five hundred each, they were still the picture of health.

"Anyway," said Simon, "I found refuge in science. In things that are concrete, present, and make sense to me."

"Yet here we are searching for an unseen element that only exists for microseconds. One which we will never actually see with our eyes and can only find in the traces it leaves behind."

"Yeah. Here we are."

Come to think of it, elemental physics was much like trying to find love. Men and women the world overthrew themselves at each other in bars, in clubs, online. All trying to cause a collision that would result in something new. They, too, would never see proof of the chemical reaction of love.

They could only measure it by the signature it left behind.

Morgan's eyes landed on the hart flower resting on a tissue on her vanity. She'd taken the flower out of her jacket after the meeting at the university. The petals had dried up now that the flower was long exposed to the elements. The stamen that surrounded the central stigma had wilted down. It no longer resembled electrons orbiting a central nucleus of protons.

"Come out tonight ..." Simon was saying.

But Morgan's attention held on the dying flower. Hadn't she picked that flower the first time she and Arthur had been caught in a compromising position?

"... few colleagues are coming over to the lab to relax after a long week and ..."

The night Arthur had proposed to her, hadn't the flowers been hanging from the flags?

"... no pressure about the job ..."

And out in the field as Arthur had held her close, they'd been standing in a patch of the flowers. Hadn't they?

The hart festival was known to heighten the pheromone levels in the town. Many assumed it was due to the flowers, like a carnal allergy. But no one had ever done tests to prove it. Morgan had never had any interest in the theory. Until now.

What if she and Arthur were having a reaction to the plant? What if this thing between them was nothing more than a hypersensitive reaction to plant dander? It made more sense to her than Arthur truly being interested in her.

"Morgan? Morgan?"

Morgan turned her attention back to her phone. "I'm sorry, what?"

"I'd like for you to come out with me and my colleagues tonight. Nothing fancy. Just a couple of cheap drinks, debates on the latest findings on String Theory with a few inappropriate jokes about engineers tossed in so we look like the cool kids. What do you say?"

She should say yes. Simon and his colleagues were far more her speed. They were her peers, not the ladies of Camelot's court.

What lay in wait for her tonight here? Would Arthur take her to one of the local restaurants where everyone knew them and would pretend not to gossip about them right in front of their faces about how the two of them didn't suit?

"I can't," Morgan said. "I'm out of your way."

"You're just outside of Caerleon? In one of the villages there? I don't mind the drive."

Morgan was about to answer. Whether it would be in the affirmative or the negative she would never know. A commotion sounded down in the belly of the castle. The fact that it rose up to her floor gave her pause.

She lived in an old castle filled with magical artifacts, charmed children, and armed knights. So, it could've been anything. But the wails of distress and shouts of panic sent a rush of cold water down her spine.

This was Camelot. No one wailed in Camelot, not from danger. No one panicked out of any real distress.

"I have to go." Morgan disconnected without saying good bye.

As she made her way out of her room, the sounds of the commotion increased. Morgan's pace picked up. She took the stairs two at a time, her heart skipping as her feet hopped over every other step on the staircase. When she reached the ground floor she froze.

It was Arthur. Morgan had never seen him lying down. He was always standing proud, balanced, and at the ready to spring into action. His eyes were always bright and alert and accusing.

But now he was prone. His eyes closed. His feet flopped out. Dark ribbons of blood covered his tunic.

Battle was constant in their world. There was always an army to face or magic that needed to be contained. But those threats almost never came inside the city limits, and never once across the drawbridge and inside the castle.

"It was the hart," said Lance. "It charged. He shoved me away to save me. I didn't see it coming. I was too busy—"

Lance choked on a cry. That sound frightened Morgan more than seeing Arthur hurt. Knights did not get choked up. Unless they were watching the World Cup. But no balls were being bandied about in the hall.

This was the work of the hart? Morgan knew the hunt was dangerous. But she couldn't recall a single instance of the magical stag actually attacking any of its pursuers.

"He's lost a lot of blood," came Gwin's voice. "We need to get him to the infirmary."

Lance and Percy carried Arthur in their arms as they headed for the stairs. Morgan stood on the last step of the stair. She knew she should move, that time was of the essence. But she couldn't get her limbs to budge as she stared down at Arthur's near-lifeless form.

Thoughts ran through her head, spiraling like electrons around an orbit. Only the atom had been blasted and the negative charges had escaped the trajectory and were now pushing the boundaries of Morgan's mind.

What if he was dying? What if he was dead? What if she never got to feel the heat of his lips press against her lips?

"Morgan? Morgan! Get out of the way."

But she couldn't move. Her mind was a mess of severed particles. Her sole attachment to the world was lying prone in front of her. Blood poured from a wound at his chest.

She needed him to be alive. She needed him to open his eyes. And then he did.

Arthur opened his eyes. The pale gray of his irises were nearly opaque. When his gaze connected with hers, they darkened, shifting into focus.

"Constant ..." His voice was hoarse. But the single word was clear.

Arthur's eyes closed, and he let out a painful sigh. The gust of his breath was like a hurricane wind to Morgan. She felt her heart plummet to the floor.

"Constance," another male voice called. "Come help Lady Gwin. Lord Arthur needs a witch's power, not these wails of women."

Morgan looked from Arthur to Sir Bors to his approaching daughter. Constance's hands already glowed with witch fire preparing to warm Arthur's body.

Morgan's palms were empty, cold. There was nothing she could do. And so she stepped aside, clearing the path up the stair.

The next hour was a fog. Morgan sat at the foot of the stair with the rest of the town as Gwin and Constance worked on Arthur.

The town always came together during a time of crisis. She felt many arms around her, many pats on the back, and murmured words of encouragement.

She didn't hear much of anything. She felt nothing at all. Until her sister tilted up her chin so that blue gaze met blue.

"He's fine," said Gwin. "We patched him up, and he's sleeping it off."

"Did he ...? Did he ask for me?"

Gwin twisted her lips in that way she did as her

erudite mind tried to twist the truth for the sake of compassion. "He didn't say much of anything."

"But he managed to say Constance's name."

Gwin grimaced. Her lower lip jerked as though she was forcing herself to keep her mouth closed on the topic.

"What? Did he say something else?"

"No," sighed Gwin. "Only that. He kept repeating her name until we got him to sleep."

Morgan looked up as a door opened and closed. It was the door to the infirmary. As Sir Bors came out, Morgan caught the slightest glimpse inside. Constance leaned over Arthur, brushing his hair from his face before applying a cloth.

Morgan's throat tightened. She tried to take in air, but it felt like the oxygen would choke her.

"We're all tired and shaken," said Gwin. "Why don't you go and get some rest. I'm sure this will all be worked out in the morning."

Yes. It likely would. Now that Arthur had come to his senses.

Morgan doubted he'd been under any outside influence when he'd courted Constance. That had been a logical decision on his part. Both she and Arthur had struggled with their attraction to each other; this thing. They both had suspected it was unnatural. And now the anomalous effects had worn off.

Well, good. She could get back to her normal life, to her regularly scheduled programming. She'd never wanted to run a castle. She hadn't planned on marrying. She wanted to be a scientist. She wanted to go to school. In fact, why wait.

"I'm not tired," said Morgan. "I'm going to go and get a drink."

CHAPTER SEVENTEEN

Fire burned in Arthur's gut, blazing bright and hot as it cauterized his wound. The blue flames scorched the four chambers, incinerating his sense of self-preservation. He reached for it. He needed the heat, wanted to taste the warmth. The sizzle and singe of it made his mouth water, his blood boil. Though the flames surrounded him, the source of the warmth was beyond his reach.

Arthur jerked awake on a strangled moan that died in his dry throat. All was dark and it took his eyes longer than normal to adjust. He knew he wasn't alone. His gaze raked the room, searching for the cold heat from his dreams.

And there it was. Just there, in the corner where

a sliver of light stole through. Cloaked in darkness, she rose and came near to him.

As she moved, the sliver of light began to separate her form from the darkness. Arthur's breaths caught pace with the pounding of his heart. He was certain the organ would burst out of its ribbed cage. He wanted more than anything to sit up in bed, but his strength failed him.

"Don't move," she said. "You're still not back to yourself."

Arthur shrank from the voice. It sounded wrong. The tone was too high. The pitch more breezy than smoky.

He collapsed back down upon the mattress only to fall into further discomfort. The pallet caught his body in a puff of softness. Where the hell was he? This was not his firm bed.

But he didn't bolt up, not when Morgan leaned over him. Instead, he recoiled. She didn't feel right. She didn't smell right. And the hair was wrong. A forest of brown surrounded eyes the color of treetops, not a dark curtain of night made for seduction under a deep blue you could only find in the corners of space.

"Please, my lord, I beg you to stay in bed."

Please? Beg? Morgan would never use such

supplicating, solicitous, imploring words. She would give direction after outlining a well-researched procedure.

It wasn't Morgan. It was Constance Bors. Lady Constance brought a cool cloth to Arthur's forehead, and he felt instantly chilled.

It took him a few tries to get the words out, and when he did, he sounded like a frog. "Where is she?"

Constance's smile was sad. "Morgan? You want to know where Morgan is?"

Arthur felt only a second's worth of shame. He'd never had to deal with rejecting the women he dallied with. They were all human. He'd never went in carnal pursuit of a witch. He owed Constance his compassion.

"My lady, I'm—"

"You don't have to explain." She wrung the rag out and placed it again on his forehead. "I always suspected there was something between you two. No one could bicker that much with no shared feelings."

Arthur frowned. There had never been anything between him and Morgan before. Not on his part.

Had there?

None of that mattered right now. Only one thing did. "Where is she?" he said again.

"Morgan was out in the hall waiting with the rest

of the community last I saw her. Poor thing. She went white when they brought you in. I'll go and get her."

"No," Arthur said. He raised himself up on the soft mattress. The cushion made him wobble instead of supporting him. "I'll go to her."

Constance huffed, but she didn't try to stop him. Arthur knew that Morgan likely would when he saw her. She'd insist he return to bed. And he would. But he'd rather be in his own bed. And he wanted her by his side there.

No one would say it was improper. He was too weak to do anything carnal. He just wanted to be alone with her. In his current state, no one would deny him that.

As his feet hit the floor, Arthur saw another figure in the corner.

"He hasn't left your side since he brought you here," said Constance as she motioned to the sleeping Lancelot. "Gwin snuck him a sleeping potion an hour ago."

Arthur would deal with Lance later. The two of them would do the whole gruff, manly apology without any song and dance that would absolve both of them their idiocy. Right now, all he wanted was Morgan.

Arthur pulled a tunic over the cotton bottoms someone had covered him with. Modesty would have to be damned. He opened the door and made his way out.

It was past dinner time. But a large number of Camelot's citizens were stuffed into the Great Hall. Children rested their sleeping heads on parents' shoulders. Chairs were shoved all around the hall. In other places, people sat on cushions or blankets or directly on the ground.

Arthur didn't make a sound at the display. His heart swelled that they'd stayed by his side during his time of need. These were his people. They knew he'd lay down his life to protect any of them. So, it shouldn't surprise him that they'd endure a little discomfort until they knew he was well.

He looked around for a dark head of hair. He must have missed her his first go around. He scanned the crowd once, then again. Still, he came up short. Finally, he spotted a blonde head of hair placing blankets over a sleeping, elderly witch.

Arthur made his way to Gwin. When she straightened and saw him, her face didn't register joy. Her features darkened at him. For the first time, he noted how much the two Galahad sisters favored.

"You should not be up," Gwin chastised.

"Where is she?"

"Morgan? She's ..." Gwin looked around. Her gaze was certain for the first second. But after a few seconds of looking left, then right, then back left again, her brow furrowed.

When the hart had raced toward him and Lance, Arthur had felt no fear, only duty. Fear crawled down his spine now at Morgan's absence.

"You're looking for Lady Morgan?" asked Sir Bors. "She left the castle over an hour ago. I saw her getting into a car and leaving the grounds."

"To go where?" said Arthur. He turned back to Gwin.

Gwin held up her hands in a placating motion. "The last thing she said to me was that she was going to get a drink."

"She could get a drink in the kitchens, or at the bar here in town. Why get in a car to leave town?"

Gwin lifted her shoulders. As she did a chime rang through the air. It was a song from a musical they'd traveled to London to see years ago. A song about a witch learning to fly and defying gravity. Arthur knew it was Gwin's ringtone for Morgan. He also knew that Loren's ring tone was a jazzy tune about a witch casting a spell over a man. Instead of placing the receiver to her ear, Gwin tapped the keys.

"She just texted me. She says she's arrived in Cardiff safe and to not wait up."

"Cardiff? What's she—" But then Arthur remembered. The night of his proposal she'd been coming from Cardiff. From the university. She'd said the Science Department was interested in her work. "She went to school as I lay on my deathbed?"

"You weren't on your deathbed," said Gwin. She took the same tone as she would with a child who swore he'd broken the leg he was still standing on.

Arthur turned a mutinous gaze on her. But like any Galahad girl, Gwin didn't scare easy. He was too weary to muster any more strength to argue. The wound was healing, but another, deeper ache spread through his limbs.

She'd left. But what did he expect? She was Morgan. She never did as he told her.

Arthur took his responsibility as lord seriously. Being the lord of this castle was the most important thing in this life, what he was born to do. The woman he chose to be his lady would need to feel the same. She certainly wouldn't leave his side when he was at his worse.

CHAPTER EIGHTEEN

The night's sky was a dark blanket. There was no space for stars to poke through. The city lights muted the celestial bodies' existence, eclipsing the powerful orbs. A light streaked across the sky, falling into the night.

Morgan knew that the term falling or shooting star was a misnomer. The dying body wasn't a star. Nor was it dying. The trail of light was simply a meteor burning up as it entered the Earth's atmosphere. The bits of dust and rock burning up as it came too close to a place it never should've dared journey.

Up ahead of her, white headlights from the opposite side of the highway came at her as she headed north. Immediately in front of her, the red of tail lights glared at her. But she didn't stop. She pressed on the gas, putting distance between herself, the place she'd orbited around her whole life and the man who had pulled her into his sphere, making her feel bright only to let her fall when she came too close. The traction burned.

Morgan pressed her fist to her chest to quell the acid sensation there. It wasn't heartburn. She hadn't had anything to eat, and her stomach wasn't grumbling.

In the end, she let the acid burn. That's what it was good for; clearing out any debris in its path. And this thing was just that; scattered pieces of something that never truly was.

She rolled down the window, allowing some of the night's cold air to slap her in the face. She couldn't catalog what she was experiencing as heartache. She hadn't given Arthur her heart.

This unquantifiable thing between them had only been in existence for twenty-four hours. And like a radioactive element, it had exploded into existence and then left without a trace.

Which was better. That meant it was a fluke. Likely unrepeatable inside a lab.

Constance was better for Arthur. She would be a

better partner. She wanted to stay home. She could offer him healing when he got hurt. Unlike Morgan who could only stand by, step out of the way, and watch helplessly.

It was late at night as she rolled through the university's gates. Bodies milled around in and out of buildings, especially the brightly lit library. The parking lot near the Science Department was full, but Morgan found a spot. Before she left the car, she pulled out her phone and texted Gwin.

She'd left in such a hurry she doubted anyone knew where she was. She didn't want to add to their worries. She only had three-percent of power left on her phone, but it was enough to send her message through before her cell died.

Morgan tucked her dead phone in her pocket and stepped out of the car. She'd pulled out heels in anticipation of spending more time with Arthur for their date. She wore them now along with a skirt that flattered her hips, and a bodice that pushed up her breasts. It wasn't exactly academic wear. But these scientists were on their downtime, so she should fit in at the local bar.

She made her way to the science building. Her toe cleavage felt the last touches of winter as she picked up her pace. Morgan pulled her wrap about her shoulders as the wind wound around her legs.

Inside the building, a night security guard sat behind the desk. "Student ID?"

"I'm not a student," said Morgan.

"My apologies," grinned the guard. "You look very young. Faculty ID, please?"

"Oh, I'm not faculty either."

The guard's smile wavered. He pursed his lips together in a grimace.

"I'm here to see Dr. Simon Accolon."

Some of the tension left his face. "Would you happen to be a Ms. Galahad?"

"Galahan," Morgan corrected.

"Oh," the man chuckled. "That would've been cool if it were Galahad." He made a sword swiping motion. Then he handed her a white plastic card on a lanyard.

Morgan accepted the card and turned it over. There was her name, Morgan Galahan, Science Department. Her thoughts scattered, a big bang in her head as she looked down at what was the start of her new trajectory in life.

After being told she needed to stay inside, to stay safe, to stay out of trouble her whole life, this card would open doors and get her into restricted areas.

The firing of the synapses of her brain rained down muting the ache in her heart.

Morgan reached out her hand and tapped the card against the closed gate. Immediately, without lecture, the doors to the inner building opened for her. She stepped onto the elevator, scanning her card again, and made her way up to Simon's floor. Stepping out of the elevator, she collided with an older man.

"I'm so sorry, Miss."

An older gentleman reached out to steady her. Morgan took one look at his gnarled fingers, she heard the creak of his old bones, and she decided that she'd better be the one to steady him. There was a mop in one hand and a bucket of dirty water at his feet.

"I'm perfectly fine," said Morgan once they both regained their balance. "Are you?"

"Oh, I'm just having a bit of trouble with a spot on the floor. Been in custodial services all my life. But working for these scientists, I'm meeting stains that are getting the better of me."

Morgan looked down at the indeterminate stain on the floor. She couldn't tell its origin, but she was sure she knew just the thing. "Just add a bit of vinegar to your cleaning solution. That'll take it right out."

The old man looked at her doubtfully.

"Trust me," said Morgan. "Acid is the great equalizer in the scientific world. It can get rid of just about any substance. You'll see."

She left the old man pondering her words and headed toward the voices down the hall. Morgan followed the voices into what appeared to be a break room. There was a large HD flat screen TV on a cart. All manner of AV equipment sat on the shelves of the metal cart, including an Xbox. Three men sat in front of the Xbox, controllers in their hands. The flashing lights from the game's explosions reflected off of all three of their prescriptive glasses.

She caught sight of Simon as he approached. "You made it."

"I did," said Morgan. "And I'm feeling a bit overdressed for … this. I thought we were going out for drinks, or something."

"I didn't say out." Simon had taken off his blazer and loosened the top button where she was certain a tie had hung earlier. "This is what scientists do when they relax."

Morgan mixed potions when she wanted to relax. She helped little witches and wizards practice their spells in her free time. Her nights were spent gossiping, mixing fruity drinks, and watching bad 80's movies with her sister and cousin.

But what did she know? The knights, the defenders of the weak and devout, had a game room. The men and squires disappeared in there after they returned from quests, or a particularly grueling day of training, to do exactly what these men of science were doing.

"You are such a geek," said one of the men. He wore a red and yellow Flash Gordon t-shirt.

"Who are you calling a geek, you nerd?" said a second man. There was a colorful scarf wrapped around his neck that reminded Morgan of Doctor Who.

"Did you know a scientist developed a mathematical equation to determine the difference between the term geek and nerd," Morgan piped in. Of course, she piped in. It was a topic she'd studied. "She plotted each of the characteristics on a graph and found that geeks are more into fandoms and collectible hobbies. Where nerds are practitioners of ideas."

The three men stopped their game and turned to stare at her. Since she had their attention, and no one else offered an opinion on her statement, Morgan decided to continue her report.

"There are similarities that both groups possess, mainly high intelligence, but they each lack social skills."

Silence reigned throughout the room. Well, except for the game's angry music questioning if they wanted to go again.

"Clearly the social aspect is proven wrong by this gathering of both geeks and nerds and—"

"Everyone," interrupted Simon, "this is Morgan Galahan. The one I told you about."

"This is the amateur with the residual effects thesis?" said the guy wearing the red superhero shirt.

In a flash, Morgan rounded on him. "Who are you calling amateur?"

Both Red Shirt and Scarf Boy reared back. They looked at each other with twin looks of skepticism.

"Do you play?" offered the third guy who wore a dark hoodie.

Looking closely, Morgan saw the third person wasn't a guy at all. As the hood fell away, a ponytail of brown, mousy hair appeared. Morgan felt a huge relief at the added estrogen in the room.

Morgan looked at the proffered game controller.

Then she looked at the game. "I used to play *The Sims*."

The de-hooded girl cringed. Redshirt and Scarf shook their heads.

"I'm pretty good at *Assassin's Creed*," Morgan offered.

"So's my dad," said Red Shirt.

"So, you're a newb," said Scarf Boy. And then, without waiting for an answer, he turned back to the game. "It's fine. Did you know that studies show that men make better gamers than women? The male species retains information better and have more dexterity than—"

A loud blast came from the television speakers. One of the on-screen character's heads exploded.

"Oops," said the girl gamer. "My bad. Guess my feminine wiles got away from me."

"You know I wasn't talking about you," said Scarf Boy. "You don't count as a girl."

Morgan saw the conflict race across the other woman's face. In the end, she stood up and tossed the controller to Simon who caught it like a hot potato. The woman motioned to Morgan and Morgan followed.

"Listen," the woman said as soon as they were out of earshot. "If you want to be taken seriously here, ditch the heels. Put your hair up and wipe the makeup off your face. No one will think you have a brain if you look like … that."

Morgan looked down at herself. "Like what?"

"Like a girl. You can get away with a name like Morgan because its gender neutral. So you'll get credit on journal articles easier."

Morgan opened her mouth, but a stiff arm with a raised palm stopped her.

"Don't talk to me about fairness or girl power or other made up crap. Science is a man's world. If you want to exist in it, you'll play by their rules. Let them win a couple of times so you'll seem less of a threat. I'm only trying to help."

"Well, thanks for mansplaining that to me, but the university headhunted me. If they want what's in my head, they'll have to take the heels too."

With one final head to toe glance over Morgan, the woman shrugged. She pulled her hoodie up. Then she rejoined the group.

Morgan looked at the group. There wasn't any extra room for her in their cluster. She searched out Simon, but his eyes were glued to the screen as he worked the controller in his hand. Morgan turned out of the room. But she didn't leave the building.

She headed to the room she'd been in before, the lab.

Her keycard gained her easy access. And there it was. The reason she was even contemplating entering this world. The cyclotron.

She walked into the control room. The LED lights were dim, the readout a flat line. Morgan ran her hand over the controls of the machine.

This was the only game she wanted to play. Unfortunately, the controller was cold and unresponsive. The accelerator beyond the glass was virtually silent.

Morgan left the panel and went over to the glass panels. Once again, she pressed her nose to the glass. A shiver ran down her spine. She was cold and her body yearned for warmth. That had to be why her mind conjured up the memory of Arthur's strong, warm bicep.

That was no longer her path. This was. She let go of the memory and focused on the machine. The machine would give up answers, eventually.

As if in response, the machine made a whirring sound. The vibration traveled through the glass sending another shiver through Morgan. The hum was warm and it raced through her, making her tingle. A red alert blasted and the LED lights turned red. Morgan jerked her hands away from the glass.

"Don't move."

She knew it was Simon's voice. He sounded close behind her. How long had he been there?

Simon's hand tightened on her, holding her still when she tried to move. Morgan wondered if she were in any danger? But just as soon as the alarm sounded, all went quiet on the screen and from the speakers.

Simon let go of her. He raced over to the controller, his eyes blazed as he read the monitors. His breath came quickly as though he'd sprinted the last few yards to the end of a marathon.

Was this it? Had there been an impact? Had two elements collided and created the new element they were looking for? If so, they wouldn't be able to see it. It would already be gone from existence. But there would be a trace. If Simon had already implemented her protocol, they would be able to see the radioactive signature.

Morgan looked down at the screen. It resembled a heart monitor after a flatline. Between the horizontal lines was a single vertical jump. There had been a huge spike, but the spike was moving down the screen as time passed. The machine was quickly returning one continuous, horizontal, flat line.

"A false alarm?" Morgan asked.

Those were known to happen in this experiment. Morgan had read up on it. Having a particle accelerator constantly firing a beam of energy to fuse two elements together resulted in the occasional misfire. But Simon's gaze was beyond disappointment from a misfire. It wreaked of desperation. Had something else gone wrong?

"Did I mess something up?" Morgan asked.

He finally met her gaze. He looked at her as though she were a puzzle. Then he laughed softly, as though the joke was on him. "For just a moment, I believed it was possible."

"It *is* possible. Sure, it's a one in a billion chance, but there is a chance."

The corner of his lip tilted up. "Odds are against it, you know."

Simon stared down at her. The light of the accelerator's beam flashed in his eyes. Even after the beam paused, a fire was still there burning bright. Morgan turned back to the accelerator unable to withstand the heat of Simon's gaze.

"You're making a mistake," said Simon. "If you don't join this team, if you stay in your small town and let them make you into something that doesn't use what's in your head, you'll regret it."

Simon lifted a hand and traced the curve of her face. She turned to face him. There was interest in his eyes. The same interest she'd seen in Arthur's eyes.

"I know," Simon continued. "My parents both tried to force me down their paths. But I've made my own way. Don't let them keep you there, Morgan. You're far too smart. Your mind could be used to further a more noble cause."

His touch sent a shiver through her. It wasn't the same as when Arthur had touched her.

"You are not what I expected, and I'm glad of it. I'm glad you're different. I want you on my team. Will you be on my team, Morgan?"

He'd said team but Morgan was smart enough to know that he was trying to recruit her for two teams; one here at the university, and a second team that would only consist of the two of them.

Simon's gaze went to her lips. The moment was ripe for a kiss. Her first kiss, with a like-minded man. A man who wasn't under the influence of a magical stag or a mind-altering pheromone. A man who didn't call out for Constance in his time of need.

Simon leaned forward. The lead nugget that

hung from the chain around his neck brushed against the skin on her chest. The abrasive rock made Morgan shiver.

If she leaned in, Simon would have the answer he wanted as their lips fused. If she leaned back, he'd misfire and miss his mark. Morgan swallowed hard and then went for it.

CHAPTER NINETEEN

At nearly two in the morning, the last of the artificial lights went out. The King's Head Tavern had gone dark shortly after midnight. It was the Witches' Brew Coffee Shop that had been the last holdout. Alcohol coursed through the veins first as an anti-inhibitor, then as a sleep aid. Whereas coffee and tea loosened the lips and kept things lively.

But eventually, the body needed rest. And so the lights of the meeting place were snuffed. The revelers went off to bed. And all was peaceful in the town of Camelot.

Arthur walked in the middle of the empty streets. His movements slow so not to awaken the pain in his chest. The wound was covered with gauze, but the edges tugged where the skin had been ripped open.

That pain was bearable. It was the deeper ache, the one he couldn't scratch and soothe with his fingers, that had him walking in the night.

Arthur's steps brought him to the city limits where they parked the town cars. There was still one missing. He stopped and stared at the vacant space.

The clock struck on the hour mark. It was officially two in the morning. A light breeze whistled through his ear. A collection of twigs tumbled out of the forest and onto the pavement.

Arthur slid his palm down until he met the scabbard that held his sword. He wrapped his fingers around Excalibur's hilt, allowing the leather to soothe his agitation. The scene had the makings of a Western standoff. The problem was, the villain in the story was late for the showdown.

Needless to say, Morgan was the villain in this story. She always had been for him. Whenever there was a mishap within the grounds of Camelot, he'd find her near.

Blue eyes flashing. Raven hair falling over her shoulders. The ends of her lush waves stopping at the tops of her breasts as though they wanted to rest and enjoy the view. Her hands would rest on voluptuous hips, hips that were meant to be hefted into a man's arms and brought down on his—

Arthur cursed under his breath. Even though she'd betrayed him, he still wanted her. When had he crossed the thin line between love and hate?

No, he'd never been at either juncture. He'd never hated Morgan. There was no aversion to her presence. No hostility toward her existence that came with hatred.

If he were honest, he could admit that he'd never truly disliked her. He'd always had a healthy respect for her intelligence and her drive and her determination. Unlike most witches, he'd never fretted over pushing her because he knew she could not only take it, she'd push him right back.

If he were brutally forthright, he'd admit that he'd liked their verbal shoving matches. Morgan had never broken. Not even when she was stripped of her magic. She'd lifted up that defiant chin and carried on.

God, that chin. He'd planned to bite that chin tonight on their first date. Not hard, just a small taste of her to whet his appetite. But instead, she was out having drinks with humans.

Oh, there was the hatred. It boiled up in him. His palm tightened on his sword, wanting, needing to slice into some libertine's flesh, especially if that blackguard had their hands on his woman.

The intensity of his feelings forced him to take a step back, off the pavement and into the grass. Looking down, he saw the distinct white and yellow of hart flowers. The wind kicked up again, and the golden specks of the flower's interior shook loose. Some of the pollen sailed through the air, other particles circled his legs and landed on the fabric.

In the distance, Arthur saw the headlights of a car. He took a few more steps back until he was in the shadows.

The car crept inside the city limits. The wheels aimed for the straight lines of the empty space but pulled just outside of the demarcations.

That didn't surprise him. Morgan was never one to color inside the lines. Why should she park there either?

The car door opened, and her feet struck the ground. He spied the tan flesh just above where her toes bunched as they met the curve of the shoe. The palm of his hand tingled again, but this time it wasn't steel he needed to touch.

Morgan shut the door and stood tall. Her black hair in sharp contrast with the moonlight. The car keys fell from her hand and hit the pavement, causing her to bend over.

Arthur's first instinct was to look away from the pull of her skirt that gave up every secret of how her ass curved. He didn't need to look away. She was his, and he'd run his sword through anyone that dared stand in the way of that fact.

His feet were already in motion toward her, to reach out and grab what was his by right, by honor, by the simple fact that he'd seen her first. But the weary sigh that left her perfect lips stopped him.

Morgan looked up at the castle. Tintagel loomed large and magical in the distance. But Morgan's expression wasn't dreamy. It was wary.

Why? Because she did not want to go to him? Because she'd decided she'd rather stay in the human world, at the university?

Too bad. That wasn't happening. Arthur took a strong step over the line, leaving behind his hatred of whomever she'd seen. That person was now a non-factor. The only thing that mattered was this thing between them. He didn't care what to call it, so long as she was his. And she would be.

At the sound of his boots on the pavement, Morgan jerked back. She turned. There was no fear in her eyes. She was home, in Camelot, where nothing and no one would harm her. What was reflected back at him was disbelief.

"Arthur? What are you doing out of bed?" Her tone was chastising, brimming with displeasure.

"What were you doing out of town?" His tone was the same, though his displeasure had crossed the boundary into anger.

He felt his nostrils flaring, his chest huffing up, fingers balling into fists. He was a powder keg that only needed the slightest strike of flint to set him off.

Morgan blinked up at him. Her head tilted slightly to the side as the steam from his huffed air torpedoed toward her. Her hands slid up her arms until they crossed over her chest. Her brows rose as she regarded him.

"Excuse me," she bristled. "First, you are not the boss of me so you can just take a step back."

He didn't. She'd lifted her chin up, defiantly. It took every ounce of control inside him not to lean down and take that bite he'd planned.

"Second, I'm a grown woman. Where I choose to go and who with is none of your business."

That snapped him back to attention. "Are you seeing someone else?"

"No." But it wasn't an emphatic denial. The oh sound wobbled and she wouldn't meet his gaze.

"It was just drinks." She tossed her hands up in clear exasperation. "With the professor who's offering me a fellowship. And yes, he's a man. But it's not like that. I mean, there was a moment. But it was awkward. And I didn't—"

Morgan stopped talking and glared at Arthur, as though he'd tricked her. She stormed past him off the pavement and onto the grass.

"Why am I telling you this. This is none of your business. My love life or lack thereof is none of your business. Go back and boss around your own fiancée."

Arthur joined her on the grass in two easy strides. "You are my fiancée. Or you will be once you come to your senses."

"Come to my senses?"

Morgan's hands landed on his chest. Arthur's heart leaped up to meet her touch. But she yanked her hand away in horror as her fingers met with the gauze that covered his wound.

Her gaze darted down lower, and she frowned. Not one of anger or irritation. Her eyes crinkled with sadness, as though she'd lost something.

Arthur followed the trajectory of her gaze, seeking to destroy whatever turned her blue. All he saw was the white and yellow of hart flowers.

"You're not in your right mind now," Morgan said. "You were when you were wounded when you called out Constance's name."

"I did no such thing."

"I was there. I was standing right there in front of you. You didn't want me. You called for Constance."

Arthur thought back. Things were hazy around those events. But he knew he never would've called for Constance. Not when everything inside him cried out for Morgan.

"I've figured it out," she said. "This thing between us was just a result of the hart flowers. We're standing on some now. It's putting you out of your mind. But you were in your right frame of mind earlier and you called out the name of the woman you truly want."

"No." Arthur reached out for Morgan and pulled her to him. "You don't get it."

Morgan struggled in his grasp, but not roughly. Whether because she was afraid of re-injuring him, or because she didn't want to leave his embrace, he didn't know. He didn't much care.

She was exactly where she was supposed to be and that was all that mattered. That and clearing up this fallacy.

"I didn't call for Constance," he said. "I was trying to explain to you what happened to me."

She held still now, waiting for the new piece of knowledge to be unveiled. Eyes bright and curious. Ever the attentive student.

"It was constant velocity," Arthur said.

"Constant velocity?"

"Yes. The hart charged me while I stood still. I lost the battle of physics."

"You were trying to say 'constant velocity', not 'Constance'?"

Arthur nodded, pulling her more snuggly into his embrace. Her hand rested just below his heart now, where the wound was. He felt the tug of skin more acutely, but that deeper ache had subsided and was nearly gone without a trace.

"Because you stood still to meet a charging hart?" Morgan was saying, turning the knowledge he'd given her over in that beautiful brain of hers. Then her blue gaze turned dark as she met his. "That was stupid. Weren't you listening to me when I explained the law?"

Arthur threw his head back and laughed. This moment was perfect. He had the woman he wanted here, safe in his arms. All was serene in the place he loved most in the world. He knew there would never be silence with Morgan.

"I can't believe you thought I wanted Constance," he said.

"Well, you did. You were set to propose to her before you got caught with me."

Arthur ran his thumb along Morgan's chin. "I wanted you."

She tilted her head up, bringing her chin in perfect alignment with his mouth. All he needed to do was lean down and take a bite.

"Then there is something wrong with your head," she said. "There's a town filled with actual witches who can help you when you're hurt, who can reinforce the covenant. I'm not one of them."

"Yet, somehow, I'm under your spell."

For the first time ever, Arthur saw Morgan Galahad at a loss for words. The moment was perfect for their first kiss. Except there was one thing that nagged him.

"How could you leave like that when I needed you?" he said. "I was on my deathbed."

"You were not dying." She sucked her teeth and rolled her eyes, much like her sister had earlier. "And there was nothing I could do for you. I've never felt so useless in my life."

"You're not useless. You're the most capable woman I know."

"I'm a witch without power. I'm a human with breasts."

Now Arthur was speechless. He was certain it would be bad form to look down and ogle her breasts. At least, not in this moment.

"What I mean is, I'm a woman in a man's field. I don't fit. Not in the human world. Not here in the magical world. Not with you. You know it's true, Arthur. You'll be back to your senses and you'll make the right decision about your future. You'll marry a witch who can run a castle, and heal you in your dangerous line of work. That's not me."

She wriggled out of his hold. Once free, she turned to walk away. He grabbed her again.

"Don't walk away from me, Morgan."

"Don't lay siege to me, my lord. You're bombarding me with this rush of emotions, and I don't know why."

His hands recaptured her chin. He cupped her face, holding her firm. She couldn't look away from him.

"There's a thing between us," he said. "You feel it."

"It's the hart. That's what makes the most sense."

"No," he said. "It was here before. It was just different. You know it's true."

Her eyes flashed fire. "You think I've been pining for you for years like some lovesick lass?"

"My father always told me that only iron can sharpen iron," he said. "You challenge me like no other."

"Are you calling me a metal now?"

"No. You're stronger than that. You're a diamond. You make me stronger, sharper."

Morgan let out a gush of air. "Such elemental words. It's making me go all fluttery inside."

Her words were spoken flatly, but Arthur heard the ring of truth in them. "This thing predates the hart. The hart may have made us look at it differently. But it will be here after the hart. It'll probably take a lifetime to solve. We can work together on it."

"Was that a research proposal?"

"Will you accept my hypothesis?"

Morgan laughed as she studied him. Arthur held still for her perusal. When she opened her mouth to speak, Arthur saw a flash of white behind her.

The hart.

It trotted past them without a care in the world.

But not before turning its head to gaze at Arthur, as though to say *Catch me if you can.*

Oh, Arthur could. He would. He would put an end to the hart's existence and prove to Morgan once and for all that this was no fluke.

"Arthur? Did you hear me? I said I would—"

"Stay here."

"—marry you. Wait? Where are you going?"

"I'm going to finish this."

Arthur tugged at the sword at his side. In the peaceful, predawn night, he brandished his sword. Excalibur's steel glinted in the moonlight, as though it were giving a sigh of relief at being of use once more. Then he dashed into the wood to put the weapon into play.

CHAPTER TWENTY

That's not how she expected it to go. But Morgan had never truly expected to be proposed to, let alone to accept said proposal. She'd definitely never imagined the intended groom to run away from her immediately after her response. A groom hightailing it a few days before the wedding? Maybe.

Arthur raced away from her now. Even though he was still injured, his powerful legs ate up the ground. He gained on the hart as the stag raced into the woods.

"I said yes," Morgan yelled after him.

He didn't turn back. His large body disappeared into the dark forest. The only sign of him was the glint of his sword that caught in the moonlight.

"Typical," Morgan muttered.

She picked her way over the earth. It was thawing as spring inched its way into the season. Her heels sunk again and again into the softening soil.

Arthur moved farther and farther away from her, but she still felt his presence. This thing between them didn't follow the normal bounds of space and time.

She'd realized that back in the lab when Simon leaned in to kiss her. As he did, she couldn't lean forward. It had felt like there was something in the way.

The thing.

Morgan wasn't entirely convinced that the hart had nothing to do with the thing. Each of the amorous escapades between her and Arthur had taken place after an encounter with the hart or its byproduct.

She kicked at one of the white flowers standing proudly in the night. It did not let go of the earth. No matter how she tried to add it all up, the hart was the constant in this equation.

But it was no matter anymore. Morgan decided right here and now that she would complete this experiment with Arthur, wherever it led them.

Which was into a dark forest in the middle of the night. Weren't there cautionary tales about this sort of thing?

She caught another flash of Arthur in the distance. His sword was drawn. She caught the glint of steel. A flash of white from the hart. And then darkness again.

Morgan groped around in the darkness, wishing she could flare up some witch fire in her palm. Or to at least use her cellphone's flashlight. But neither her hands or her phone had power. And so she pressed forward in the dark.

"Arthur?" she called out.

"Stay back," came his low, animalistic growl.

"Come here."

"Morgan, do as you're told."

"Seriously? If this is how this relationship is going to start, I foresee many problems."

Strong arms grabbed her from behind. She was pulled inside taut muscles, enveloped in a spicy scent. She didn't jump or jerk away. She was already coming to know his touch, his smell, the feel of him.

"Foresee problems?" Arthur said into the cone of her ear. "You've been a thorn in my side for a century. But right now, you're going to mind what I tell you and stay put."

Arthur tucked Morgan into a tree. He leaned forward, his face nearly upon hers. There was no obstruction between them. The air was free and clear.

Morgan leaned in. Arthur held her back. His throat worked and his gaze stayed glued to her lower lip. He ducked in for the quickest, most unsatisfying peck ... on her cheek.

"Seriously?" she said.

"I'll make it up to you."

Morgan opened her mouth to protest, but he was already beyond her reach. Walking backward toward the moon; moonwalking. Swaggering in the moonlight was a better description.

"Be a good girl," he called. "Stay put."

Morgan was too hypnotized by the sway of his hips, the power of his thighs, the broadness of his shoulders to protest the command.

Arthur grinned, as though he knew exactly what she was thinking. He winked and then turned, coming face to face with the hart.

The magnificent stag stood just twenty yards away from them. Its white coat shined like a star in the night. A cloud of hot air streamed from his flaring nostrils. It pawed one hoof at the ground like a bull preparing to charge.

Arthur brandished his sword. He held it across his body like a red cape. All was still as man and beast took their marks for the dance, only waiting for their cue.

Morgan didn't hear the battle hymn start. She felt as though she were thrown in the midst of a tenor's aria as Arthur's boots stomped the ground and the hart's hooves split the earth. When knight met stag, the crescendo was loud enough to silence the stars.

The light of impact was so brilliant that Morgan had to shield her eyes. It took precious long seconds for the beams to dim before she could unshield her eyes.

When she did, she saw a gruesome scene. Arthur lay on the ground. Blood covered his chest where his wound had reopened.

Morgan rushed to his side. He lay unresponsive on the forest bed. She used her hands to press at the wound, but the blood continued.

Her brain worked. She knew he was losing too much blood and if it continued there wouldn't be enough to keep his heart beating. She knew it outside of logical fact because she felt her own heartbeat slowing down.

Morgan needed to get help, and soon. But the

time it would take her to get to the castle were precious moments that would certainly leave him dead. She didn't have the strength to carry or drag him. Even technology failed her when she looked at her uncharged phone.

For the second time tonight, she was left helpless and impudent. She wanted to scream. She wanted to pound at the cold earth. A stream of heat hitting her cheek had her lifting her head.

The hart loomed over her. Its dark eyes intent. Its bared teeth grinding as it took steady steps toward her.

Excalibur protruded from the hart's side. The wound struck true but not in a place that would quickly end the stag's life. And it was very clear what the magical beast was intent on doing in its final moments.

Too bad Morgan wouldn't go down without a fight. She was a Galahad girl, after all. They never did what was expected.

She looked around for options; rocks, branches, weeds, a dead cell phone, her heels. Before she could complete her inventory of tools of destruction, her gaze was drawn to the hart's huffs of breath coming through its flaring nostrils.

The clouds of air sparkled. In fact, they weren't

clouds at all. They were spheres; round, globular masses with colors circling within their orbit. Morgan stood, taking a step forward to get a closer look.

With each breath, she saw constellations form. When the mist left the hart's nose it began as a red blast, that turned to a yellow mass, and finally a white mist before disappearing. Next a purple puff, to a blue fog, and a pink vapor. In the space of seconds, galaxies came to life and died in the hart's exhalations.

She needed to get closer. Something urged her closer. Looking up, she met the hart's gaze again. The menace had evaporated and was replaced with discernment.

Morgan knew the look well. It was the same look she saw when she looked into little Annora Godfrey's eyes when she explained atomic structure. Annora's eyes would light up with the new knowledge. Just as Morgan's eyes would light anytime someone showed her something new. And now, looking into the glassy eyes of a magical stag, Morgan saw a kindred spirit.

The hart bowed his head so that Morgan could see clearly into his eyes. What she saw took her breath away. In the light of the hart's eyes she saw long and intertwining strings, all gathered in a loose ball of connections.

The hart stepped forward, giving her an even closer look. She felt the tension in his haunches as a thickening trickle of blood left the spot where the blade was embedded in his flesh. Morgan knew instinctively that it craved her understanding. That understanding came swiftly and nearly overwhelmed her.

The hart allowed her a window into its inner being. Bright balls of light swirled in what looked like chaos, but Morgan saw form. She saw the formation of hydrogen with its singular proton and orbiting electron. The bright balls of light continued adding to the orbit.

There went phosphorous with its fifteen bright balls of protons gathered at the center of fifteen swirling lights of electrons. After a while, tungsten burned bright with its seventy-four protons bulging in the middle of seventy-four lapping electrons.

The lights continued piling on and on. This was the Periodic Table of Elements as no one had ever seen it before. There was a pregnant pause as ninety-two protons filled the nucleus of uranium, what once was thought the last naturally occurring element. After uranium, scientists had begun synthesizing elements, creating them in labs. Morgan held her breath, wondering what the hart would show her of the next line on the Periodic Table.

She wanted to laugh at what the hart showed her next. The human scientists had the right of it after all. Inside the hart's eyes, she witnessed the bright lights of atoms crashing together to form new bonds. With the heat of the hart's magic, the bonds held.

One hundred nineteen protons, all held together in a perfect union with the magical magnetism of the hart. Like ingredients put in a pot to come to a brewing blend, add a little fire and the bond held. Like magic.

Exactly like magic.

Morgan had found it. Element 119 was magic. It made perfect sense. Magic and science converged to form something new.

"Morgan?"

Arthur's voice was feeble and weak. She turned to see him struggling to his feet, reaching out to her, readying to protect her even through his mortal wound.

Blood poured from his chest, spilling all the elements inside him. She had to stop it. To reinforce his bonds. Morgan turned to the hart.

The hart huffed, as though it were put out by the plea that had yet to leave Morgan's lips. It took another step closer to her. Behind Morgan, she heard Arthur shouting, pleading with her to back away.

Instead of listening to him, she listened to her logical mind. The math was on her side in this. A second later, she confirmed that she was right.

The hart lifted its head until Morgan's hand rested on the ruff of its heart. Morgan was no stranger to the outdoors and the animals found there, but the hart's flesh was not the firm sinew of any stag she'd ever encountered on the grounds of Camelot. Her hand went straight through flesh, blood, and muscle to meet with ... She had no idea what.

It was warm. A burning furnace. A funneling tornado.

Just like magic.

She felt the same heat engulf her free hand; warm fire that tugged at her like a determined storm. Arthur.

It all took the space of a heartbeat. She knew because a second later she was being yanked into Arthur's arms. His eyes wide with fear.

"Morgan?"

Morgan's face came against his bare chest. His bare, healed, chest. The blood was gone. The skin reknit, with only scar tissue to mark the spot.

Morgan pressed her lips to Arthur's skin. She felt his heartbeat answer her with a strong thump. Then she was being yanked forcibly away from him.

"Why would you do something like that?" he growled at her. "Will you never mind what I tell you?"

"Um, I just saved your life." She placed her hand on his chest.

He glared down at her fingers. Then his darkened features brightened into awareness. Slowly, he unfurled her fingers from his chest.

"The hart and I saved your life," said Morgan. "He showed me how. He showed me what I've been looking for. He showed me how to form the missing element. I was right. It's not the blast. It's in the residual effects. That's what holds things together."

"I have no idea what you're talking about," Arthur said.

Morgan didn't try to explain it. You had to see it to believe it. The hart brought things together that wouldn't normally stick.

Skin torn asunder. Flowers in the winter time.

Morgan, the feminist scientist, and Arthur, the valiant knight.

"It's done," said Arthur. "The hart is dead."

Like all radioactive elements, the hart's life was impermanent. When it showed its true nature, it went out in a burst of light. Looking down, Morgan saw that there was nothing left of the hart but his antlers.

"It's not dead," said Morgan. "Energy never dies. It can't be destroyed. It just takes a different form. No, that's not right. It went to another realm of—"

But she didn't get to finish the sentence. Arthur captured her lips in a searing kiss. His mouth on hers warmed her in a way the hart never could. The bursts of light behind her eyes paled in comparison to what the hart had shown her, to anything she'd seen under a magnifying glass. The chemical reaction between her and Arthur would power a city, or raze it to the ground with its force.

"You said 'yes' earlier," he said when he pulled away.

"Hoping I'll take it back now?"

"You'll never get another opportunity. We're out of the experimental phase. You and I are now a fact."

"I can accept that conclusion."

CHAPTER TWENTY-ONE

Morgan's hand was warm in his, as though the hart's magic still connected them. Arthur had nearly lost his life mere hours ago when he'd tried to murder the beast.

His homicidal instincts were not for the notoriety that came with felling the hart. Arthur had wanted to run the stag through for cockblocking him. He'd felt certain that once the stag was dead, this thing between himself and Morgan would be validated. Wasn't karma funny?

He'd been falling into darkness after colliding with the hart. The pain of the impact had pulled him under swiftly and efficiently like a tidal of darkness. But he'd managed to surface one last time, and when he did, he flailed to keep his head above water.

Morgan had knelt before the hart. The beast had been ready to strike. But then it didn't.

Arthur had watched as the hart's entire countenance changed as it regarded Morgan. Annoyance washed from its eyes. Its gaze brightened with surprise. It had appeared as though a smile kicked up the corner of the stag's muzzle. And finally, it lowered its head, in surrender, or maybe in reverence, to her.

It was the same trek Arthur had taken with the confounding woman. And just like Arthur, the hart had taken the necessary steps toward her to allow himself to be wrapped around her finger. Something had transferred between woman and beast and that thing brought Arthur back to life and foiled his plans.

He'd attempted to prove that the hart was not between them. Instead, it was the hart that brought them inextricably back together.

Tingles flared up Arthur's arm as Morgan's thumb brushed the fleshy part of his wrist. The softness of her body pressed into his side turned him hard. The small sigh that escaped her perfect lips coiled him tight. Anymore contact and he'd spring an embarrassing leak.

He was operating on no sleep, a desire fogged brain, and the adrenalin of nearly dying twice in one day and it left him haggard. Yet he wouldn't trade a second of it if it brought him to this place with Morgan standing beside him.

Luckily, the fierceness in her gaze eclipsed the lukewarm reception they were currently receiving in the Great Hall. They'd arrived moments ago after lingering in the forest prior to breakfast being served. The entire town was present as Arthur made their happy announcement.

The clatter of silverware on porcelain plates halted. Conversations muted. A sea of faces turned respectfully toward them. Silence continued to reign as heads tilted and swiveled as though they were waiting for him to say something more.

"Did she actually accept him this time?" said a voice.

It was a child's voice. Arthur knew because he heard a hush that only a mother could give. He found the face of little Giles Fletcher.

The kid looked indignantly at the finger covering his mother's lips that had been used to shush him.

Arthur couldn't be upset. It was a perfectly valid question.

"Yes," Morgan answered. "I accepted Arthur's proposal for the great honor that it is."

Morgan punctuated her statement with a squeeze of his hand. Another flare of liquid energy shot through Arthur's system, just like it had last night when his life essence had poured out of him. She'd managed to pour the hart's essence into his body and heal him, make him whole, a new man.

"Did he get down on his knee again?" asked Annora Godfrey.

"Better," grinned Morgan. "He formatted the proposal as a logical equation that led to an inevitable conclusion."

Annora sighed, placing her hand over her heart. Gwin chuckled, ducking her head which didn't mute the sound. Everyone else looked around baffled.

"I thought she was a lesbian," someone said in a hoarse whisper.

"What's a thespian?" asked little Giles.

"An actress," answered his mother.

"You're a lucky man." Lance approached Arthur, hand outstretched.

Arthur looked at the man's open palm. He knew what it meant. It was more than congratulations. It was an *I'm sorry for not having your back while a magical beast charged us both.*

From Arthur, it was an *I should've considered how my decision might affect your future happiness.*

Then came a *Yeah, that was a dick move.*

Followed by a *Don't forget, I was nearly gutted for you, asshole.*

And finally, a *So, we're cool?*

And lastly, a *Yeah, we're good.*

With a grunt and a manly nod, the two men squashed their beef.

"To the happy couple." Lance raised his goblet of orange juice. The fruity beverage sloshed over the sides of the cup as it went high into the air.

Applause was a trickle through the tables spread out in the hall. Percy and Tristan stood, raising their goblets and a resounding cheer. This was echoed by the young ones scattered throughout the bunch. The young couple who Arthur had forced into engagement stood next, arms entwined as they raised their glasses. And finally, the adults joined in, and doubt auto-tuned into true good wishes before the raucous cheering died down to normal a boisterous volume.

Arthur turned from the crowd to look down at Morgan, his intended bride. He was certain a light shone between them. The thing growing and pulsing like a living entity. Bright and grasping as a new babe searching for its first taste of succor.

Only to have it tugged away from him. Arthur held firm to Morgan's hand as a crowd of women swooped in, cooing over her and trying to tug her attention away.

"Congratulations, my dear," said one. "You've finally got your man after all this waiting."

Morgan shook her head, dark locks swaying back and forth to draw a clear line. Before she could get out any denial, more women swarmed in.

"There's much to discuss about the wedding," said one. "It's going to be a grand affair."

"Oh, it can be something simple." Morgan looked to Arthur for support. Her fingers pressed into his more firmly as the women continued to tug at her.

"Nonsense. It's been too long since Camelot's had a grand wedding."

"There will be lots for you to plan, my dear."

"Have you told your mother yet?"

Gwynfhar Galahad was safely tucked away in Florida at a castle stronghold near Disney World. She had been a force to be reckoned with a century ago when she'd set her sights on her two girls marrying the Pendragon boys. She'd come away one and zero. She would be thrilled that her record would now be undefeated.

Morgan's grip went slack at the mention of her mother. That allowed the women to get a hold of her. "Save me," she pleaded. "You promised to protect me from harm."

Arthur looked between his intended and the crowd of biddies. Magical harts, dragons, trolls, he'd step in front of any of them for her. The town women? He'd shove her in front of them to save himself in a heartbeat.

Arthur let his intended bride go and waved as she was carted away as a sacrifice. Her blue gaze flashed murder at him. He chuckled at the threat.

Taking one of the many empty seats, he found himself surrounded by his knights. He'd have to start filling those vacant seats soon. But it could wait until after the wedding.

"Any news on the Templars?" said Arthur.

"This is your time of celebration," said Tristan. "You won the hart hunt."

"Technically Morgan did. She's the one that brought the stag down." They'd brought the stag's rack back to the castle. The antlers would be mounted in a place of honor, but the honor would be Morgan's. "Now, I need to know she's safe."

"We've already told you," said Lance. "There's a Templar after the Philosopher's Stone. But it's a pipe dream. Humans will never be able to transmute things. Even Morgan said so."

"Do we know where this man is?" asked Arthur.

"He's gone to ground," said Lance. "If he surfaces, our informants will get word to us."

"Interesting story about that one, though," said Percy. "He bagged a Banduri a few decades ago. Even went so far as to marry her. Can you imagine the children?"

Arthur couldn't. Templars considered Banduri fake witches, but witches nonetheless. How a romance could evolve from two such opposing sides baffled him.

"But like we said," Percy continued. "Malegant Accolon is not a concern at present. Though seriously, anyone who calls themselves Malegant needs to be locked up."

"Face it, Arthur," said Lance. "This is a time of peace."

They were right. Peace is what Arthur wanted so that he could enjoy his new bride. He needed peace for his wedding. He needed that peace to hold weeks after the wedding night while he got to know his bride properly. The thought of stripping Morgan down to her bare flesh and curves once again tightened his body.

"Easy there," said Lance.

Arthur looked down to see that his knuckles were white as they gripped the table.

"Never imagined her for you," said Percy. "Figured someone more docile, quiet, and nurturing."

Arthur would've thought the same. Truth was he hadn't truly contemplated marriage, not until Morgan was in his arms behind the family flags. Now, he couldn't think of anyone else being his betrothed.

"Lady Morgan is nurturing in her own way," said Tristan. "She loves to teach the children."

"How to blow things up," said Percy. "She's always been my favorite."

"She's quiet when she has a book or a beaker in her hand," said Tristan.

"And who wants a docile chit in the bedroom, eh?" said Percy.

Arthur gave Percy a stony glare. It didn't cow him. Percy's grin spread.

"I think our fearless leader might be in love," cooed Percy.

"We don't talk about any witch in that way," said Arthur.

The witch in question had made her getaway and was headed to him. Arthur held out his hand to her and like a magnet, she came to him. He felt the pull between them, that invisible force snapping them back into place.

"I will murder you in your sleep if you do that to me again," were her words of devotion.

Arthur chuckled as he tucked her into the chair beside him. Just barely stopping himself from pulling her onto his lap.

"Am I allowed at the big boys' table now?" she said.

"You're to be my wife." He loved the sound of that. "Your place is at my side wherever I might be."

"Does that mean I get to come into the Throne Room? Or the weapons room? Oh, can I learn the secret handshake?"

"There is no secret handshake," said Arthur.

"Loren said there was," said Morgan.

"She lied," said Lance.

"She did try to institute one," said Tristan. "But she kept changing it and no one could remember."

Morgan and the knights fell into an easy conversation. People continued to stop by and congratulate them. Arthur kept a firm hold on Morgan, not allowing any more old biddies to pull her away again. Not that he was afraid of being murdered by her in his sleep. Because he simply wanted her there.

He watched her laugh, watched her eat, watched her listen to those around her with attentiveness. She relaxed back into him as she did. It felt natural. Perhaps this was a love match? Whatever it was, he was happy and he had no intention of letting her go.

CHAPTER TWENTY-TWO

"Why can't this just be a casual affair? You know, a barbecue out on the jousting fields. Dancing in the dining hall. Didn't a few of the squires form a band? They could play."

Aghast didn't begin to describe the looks that the elder women of Camelot gave Morgan.

"You'd have such a momentous occasion as the union of our Lord be done in the backyard with plastic cups and spicy tomato sauce?"

Morgan knew the answer to that question was no. Though it actually sounded pretty good to her.

"Isn't this wedding my day?" she tried instead. "Isn't this about me and Arthur? Not the whole town?"

The women looked from her to each other as

though she were spouting an alien tongue.

"I'm going to be terrible at this, aren't I?" she said to Gwin after the women released her to plan her wedding on their own.

"You are going to be brilliant like you always are," said Gwin. "They'll simply have to get used to your flair. You're the Lady of the Castle now."

The first part of Gwin's statement had sounded upbeat and light. But the second part, the part where she signed over the duties she'd held for the last half-century, sounded leadened.

"Am not," said Morgan.

"Are too," Gwin chided, her voice still caught in the downbeat. "You're marrying the Lord of the Castle, which makes you the Lady."

"I don't have any magic to reinforce the covenant."

As she said it, Morgan's attention went to her gut, that place where all witches' and wizards' magic resided. Her gut had been hollow for months. But today it was warm, not burning and brimming as it had been every day of her life as a powerful witch. The only thing that had changed in her life was her feelings for Arthur. She supposed that now he would take up that space there.

"That's where people are mistaken." Gwin shook

her head. "The magic is in the bond, not the person. And it's clear that you and Arthur have forged a very strong, very special bond."

Gwin's look was a bit green. Morgan never knew her sister to envy anyone or have an ounce of jealousy. She was the most giving and caring person likely in the universe. Which was the reason she hadn't married the man she truly loved.

Gwin's marriage to Merlin had been arranged. She'd had little choice in it, down to the color of her dress. She'd gone along willingly, repeating her mother's words that this was for the good of their society and that Merlin needed her.

All of which was true. The marriage was good for Camelot in bringing people together. Merlin did need her healing powers. Beneath her smile, Morgan knew her sister secretly would've preferred a different path. Just as they didn't speak of Merlin, they also didn't speak of Gwin's feelings for Lancelot.

Morgan knew that her sister flourished in the role as Lady of the Castle. And so Morgan would not take her one true happiness from her.

"Lady of the Castle is your role. You married the eldest Pendragon. You're still his wife. You both made and kept your vows. You'll keep that title even after he dies."

Conflict deepened the grooves of Gwin's pretty features.

"You know I'm not cut out for that job," said Morgan. "I tried to tell Arthur."

"I think Arthur mostly wants you as a wife."

Morgan felt a blush rise to her face. She would be Arthur's wife soon. She knew the kiss they'd shared was only the beginning. She'd felt his powerful body against hers and knew there was so much more to the new role she'd agreed to take.

"Do you realize that Lady of the Castle is a job where you have to sleep with someone to get the gig?" Morgan chuckled.

Once again, Gwin turned green. But Morgan suspected there was no jealousy this time.

"I take it you didn't enjoy the bed sports part of your marriage duties?" said Morgan.

"Morgan, that's personal."

"It's gonna happen to me soon. You have to tell me what to expect."

"Mother will do that."

"Mother already did that."

They both cringed at the memory of their mother's sex education lessons. Unlike in the human world, the talk was a standard and expected practice with all young witches. Somewhere along the lines of history, human women were taught that their bodies were shameful. That knowledge never passed to witches and they learned that their bodies, like their magic, were gifts that they had to master.

Still, their mother, Gwynfar, was not the ideal teacher. She was very clinical in her explanations. While Morgan knew the physical ins and outs of coitus, she had no clue about the emotional or spiritual side. And wasn't that funny. The scientist who preferred facts above all else craved experiential knowledge.

"Were you overcome with passion that first time?" asked Morgan.

"I ... We ..."

"Or was it disgusting? Did it hurt?"

Gwin fidgeted, looking away from Morgan.

"That bad?" Morgan chewed at her lip. "The first time is said to be uncomfortable. But they say it gets better with time."

Now Gwin chewed her lip and fluttered her hands as though she were looking for something, anything else to occupy herself.

"It didn't get better for you, did it? The bastard. I bet Lance would've been a great lover."

As if on cue, the man in question turned a corner. He walked beside Constance Bors. Lance leaned down to Constance, tilting his ear toward her mouth. After Constance spoke, Lance pulled away with a grin on his lips. They both laughed and continued on their way down the hall, neither having seen the Galahad sisters.

"What kind of lover Sir Lancelot is, or is not, is none of my business." Gwin smoothed out the pleats of her skirts. Then, without another word, she folded her hands at her middle and walked in the opposite direction of the couple.

Morgan stood still. Her mind focused on a single direction. The whole idea of a wedding night was ridiculous. When the bride and groom left the wedding party, the entire guest list knew exactly what they were getting up to. No wonder there was performance anxiety. At least no one displayed bloodied sheets the morning after the wedding to prove a woman's virginity as they'd done in medieval times.

The planning of the wedding was already getting out of hand. The whole day of the event—or weekend if the women of the town had their way— would be exhausting. It would have nothing to do with her or Arthur. It would be about everyone else, as Morgan was summarily informed moments ago.

Everyone had witnessed her first proposal and it

had been a disaster. Her second proposal, which had been perfect, had been about her, and only she had been witness. Her first time with Arthur in bed should be a private matter that no one knew about.

The sun was setting out of the picture window in the Great Hall. Morgan saw a trickle of bodies headed toward the castle from the path that led into the town square. The dinner bell would ring soon. She had just enough time to enact her plan.

Morgan hurried to her room. Did a quick wash. Took considerably longer to find an outfit and change before slipping out of her room.

She headed for the stair, but she didn't go down. Instead, she went up. Up to a corner of the castle she'd never once visited before.

It was an ordinary looking door. Oak maybe? Old but not a single sign of rot. It looked like it was still living and soaking up nutrients from the soil beneath the castle.

The door was unlocked. Of course, it was unlocked. The great Arthur had very little fears, to begin with, and definitely nothing to fear inside his home. Morgan shut the door behind her and looked around the room.

It was as though she'd walked outside into the forest on a cool day. The interior of the room was done in deep brown and mahogany. The posts of the four poster bed reached up to the ceiling and stretched down to the floor, as though it was carved from the same tree as the door. A deep green blanket covered the bed.

All around the room were accents of colorful tapestries; lush reds, vibrant yellows, stunning oranges. It reminded Morgan of the interior of a sheik's tent. Which was fitting since Arthur was the ancestor of desert nomads.

Morgan heard the shower stop. She hadn't noticed that the water had been running. The patter of drops had fit in the oasis of a room. Now that she heard Arthur padding around behind the bathroom door she lost her nerve.

Too late. The door to the bathroom opened and Arthur stepped out. Feet bare, torso glistening, only a damp towel wrapped around his waist to preserve his modesty.

He ran a second towel through his hair, which was why he didn't see her immediately. When he pulled the towel down his face and over his beard, his gaze finally met hers.

He didn't startle. There was some surprise in his gray gaze, tinged with a hint of curiosity. He tossed the hair towel back into the bathroom and turned to her, smiling patiently, waiting for her to speak.

"I've made a decision," said Morgan.

Arthur lifted an eyebrow and sighed. He padded over to her, stalking her slowly like a big cat. She hadn't noticed how big he was until this very moment. His broad shoulders filled her vision. The heat coming off of him turned the room humid.

"It's too late to back out," he said as he prowled.

"Oh, no. No. You're stuck with me." She took a deep breath, her lungs filling with the spicy scent of his soap. "I've decided I don't want to wait."

"To be married? We can't elope. The town wants a grand wedding."

Arthur captured a strand of her hair between two fingers and rubbed. He'd kissed her just the other night. He'd held her close this morning in the dining hall. But watching him roll a few strands of her hair between his thumb and forefinger somehow constricted her chest, making her breaths go shallow and her pulse race. She may have imagined it, but she thought she saw sparks between them, like the connection was a living, breathing thing.

"I'm not talking about the ceremony," she said.

Arthur was busy concentrating on the curl of her hair. Slowly, realization dawned. He let the strands of her hair slip through his fingers, and he took a step back.

"It's supposed to hurt the first time," said Morgan. "Not because of the woman's hymen. That's an erroneous belief. I know it's because the penis entering the body for the first time is an adjustment."

Arthur choked as though he'd taken a swallow of something spicy and it went down the wrong pipe. He took a couple more steps back until the backs of his knees hit the edge of his bed. He dropped down onto the mattress as though hit by a truck.

"My body will need to stretch to learn to accommodate you," Morgan said. "My proposal is that we begin the process now so I'll be stretched enough to enjoy the actual wedding night."

"Your research is flawed." Arthur found his voice. "I would never hurt you, Morgan."

"Prove it." Morgan made her way over to him.

Arthur held up his hands as though to ward her off. "I am not taking your virginity before we say our vows."

"One," Morgan held up her index finger, "I'm sharing this experience with you. You're not taking or plundering my bounty like some carnal conqueror. Two," she added her middle finger to her index finger, "we can say vows now if it makes you comfortable."

Arthur said nothing.

"What is it with men and virgins?" Morgan huffed. "My virginity doesn't belong to you. It's not a commodity. I know how to pleasure myself, you know. I've grown up around witches."

Now, he groaned. He turned his body away from her, but there wasn't anywhere he could escape. To his left and right were the posts of his bed. Behind him was the vast expanse of his mattress. Standing before him was the woman who was destined to join him in that bed someday. Morgan was determined this would be that day.

"I don't like the unknown," she said. "I don't like things beyond my control. Can't we just get it over with now? So I'll know what to expect later."

"Get it over with?" Now he faced her. Indecision replaced with righteous indignation. "When I'm inside you, I plan to stay for days."

"That's not possible," she said. "The average erection lasts thirteen minutes."

"I'm no average man."

"I say again; prove it."

CHAPTER TWENTY-THREE

This was not how Arthur had planned for his night to go. He'd taken a cold shower trying to chill the fever that had taken over him since that kiss. That kiss when he'd finally taken her into his arms and had the first of many tastes.

Arthur had planned to take it slow with her. She was an innocent, though she'd kissed him like she'd been hungering for him for years, centuries.

It had been first a nibble. Then she'd taken a bite out of him. And now she wanted the full course. That was not on the planned menu.

But when did anything ever go as planned with Morgan? The witch never did as she was told. Well, she'd have to learn to mind him now that she would be his wife. And that lesson would start now.

Morgan reached out to touch him.

Arthur caught her hand. Was it proof she wanted? He'd give her a few facts and then leave the problem to be solved on their wedding knight.

"Be a good girl," he said.

Those lush lips turned down in a frown, making Arthur's mouth water. With his free hand, he captured her face. With her cheek in the palm of his hand, he pulled her to him and took a bite of his own.

Her lips were parted. She had been ready to say something, to offer a retort to his command. But it was lost in the wanton tangle of tongues, in the light touching of teeth.

With the hand at her chin, Arthur pulled her closer. Bending and twisting her head to his will. With the hand that held hers, he placed her palm over his heart so that she would feel its powerful pounding and come to understand just how strong his desire for her was. More importantly, that she would understand the enormous amount of will he exerted to control it.

But she was Morgan. He should've known that if he went right, she'd charge ahead. So as he focused on the north, she went south.

Curious fingertips poked at the top of his towel.

The pad of her thumb rubbed at the line where his bare belly met the trail of coarse hairs.

Arthur growled. The low, deep rumble shook loose Morgan's fingers, and he caught her free hand. He held it captive as he glared down at her. But the growl wasn't filled with menace. It was desire that had burst from him. The tight leash of control slipped a few notches, leaving his defenses woefully lacking.

"Morgan," he warned.

"What?" Her brow pinched in genuine puzzlement. "You said you'd prove it. We'll need your tool for this experiment."

That caught him off guard. A chuckle escaped him. Forget keeping him on his toes. This woman would constantly knock him back on his heels.

"I've never seen a naked man," she said. "Outside of pictures and statues. And little boys that I've babysat for."

"I'm not a little boy."

"Prove it."

He was a grown man. But he couldn't resist the challenge from this woman. He'd show her his. Once she saw how eager he was to make her acquaintance, she'd back off.

Arthur let the towel drop.

Morgan took a step back.

Arthur clenched his hands to keep from reaching out to her. His erection showed no such manners. It sprang toward her, the tip straining to cover the distance she'd placed between them.

But Morgan hadn't run away. She'd only taken the necessary step to look down and take him in. "Well, now. That is impressive."

Arthur had never blushed a day in his life. But the taut flesh of his groin did. The color was beyond a pale blush of pink, it was nearing bloody red.

"I suppose it's my turn now," she said.

Before Arthur could launch a protest—and in all honesty, he wasn't exactly sure if that was what he would've done—Morgan reached for the tie of the robe she wore and tugged.

The fabric fell off her shoulders revealing honey golden skin. Arthur's eyes were immediately drawn to the dark brown nipples at her chest. They pebbled like the topping of a decadent treat. He hadn't even touched her, yet the sugar rush went straight to his head, and he nearly lost his mind. Nearly.

"I know it's hideous." Morgan's hands went to cover the scar at her belly.

Arthur's jaw clenched at the sight of it. His own

brother had been responsible for that mark there when she'd been cut with the weapon that stole her magic. Arthur pried her palms away from the bit of flesh. Heat met the backs of his knuckles when he touched her torn skin.

"I know I'm not flat in all the right places and bumpy in some other places."

With great difficulty, Arthur lifted his gaze from said bumpy places to watch the movement of Morgan's lips. His brain was truly muddled. The words she formed weren't making any sense.

"My mother will be sure to put me on a diet before the wedding, so things should smooth out somewhat by then. And I'll try to keep it tight, but I actually like bread and believe that the only way to eat a tomato is on a bed of pasta, not lettuce and—"

Arthur silenced her with a kiss. He let his lips communicate just what he thought about her bared flesh. His tongue told her how much he wanted to taste every inch of it.

"You're perfect," he said when he let her take in air.

"Are you sure?"

"I've never wanted anyone, or anything, more in my life more than I want you," he said. "I vow to you my blood and my bone. I give you my body, that we two might be one. I give you that which is mine to give. I give you my spirit until the day your life is done."

He'd had a plan. He'd planned to teach this woman who was boss. He'd planned to show her who was in command. And yet again, like every time he came face to face with Morgan Galahad, he found himself on his knees and at her mercy.

He was on his knees now. A dark triangle of a gift was before his eyes. Arthur leaned forward and used his tongue to unwrap it.

Morgan gasped, jerking her hips back.

Arthur slid his hands up the backs of her thighs. He cupped her full ass, holding her in place. "Be a good girl."

This time she didn't protest. A spark lit her blue eyes, like a lightbulb shining from the inside out seeking clarity. He would show her. He'd hide nothing.

She'd asked him for proof; proof of his prowess, proof his lovemaking would bring pleasure and not pain; proof that the vows he'd just made he'd hold to the end of his days. Arthur dipped his head and set about proving his position.

At the first swipe of his tongue, Morgan's knees buckled. Arthur held her upright, slipping his tongue deeper into the folds of her sensitive flesh. His lips found the tight bud of her pleasure and he sucked, pulling it into his mouth and flicking his tongue mercilessly.

Morgan braced her hands on his shoulders. And finally, for the first time in their lives, she gave into him.

Her sweet nectar flowed over his tongue. Her tremors radiated from her core. Her thighs shook. Her knees bent. She collapsed in a puddle into his arms.

Arthur scooped up his treasure. He rose on steady legs and lifted her onto the bed. He lay her soft form onto his firm mattress and then covered her with his hard body.

She uttered no protest. She offered no analysis. She simply opened for him.

Her gaze was wide and trusting. Her arms uncrossed from her chest, leaving her heart bare. Her knees parted, pink flesh glistening as it continued its aftershocks of pleasure.

His patience had been tried. He'd said his vows. Arthur could wait no longer. He took himself in hand, preparing to take the final step of this lifelong journey. But first, he couldn't help himself.

"Morgan."

"Yes, Arthur?"

"It's been thirteen minutes," he said. "I'm still standing."

Realization was slow to straighten her brow. She smiled sheepishly. "I stand corrected."

"You need to understand; once I'm inside you, you're mine."

"I thought I already was yours."

"There was a slim chance I'd have let you go. Caveman tendencies will kick in once I breach your treasure. I will never let you go. Do you understand me?"

One of Morgan's hands went to his heart. The organ beat so powerfully, it moved her fingers with each thump. The other hand she moved to his cheek. The warmth of her fingers permeated the thick hair of his beard, and he felt her touch deep inside him. It was all the consent he needed.

Inch by inch, he made his way inside her warm and welcoming flesh. When her untried channel constricted his advance, Arthur reached down and rubbed at the swollen flesh at the apex of her sex. Even though the nub had given her pleasure just moments ago, the tight bundle of nerves eagerly reacted to his continued attention. With each contraction her core pulled him farther and deeper into her channel, claiming him as her own.

Arthur had never pondered the origin of the universe. He knew for a fact that there was a god and she was a woman. Or at least humanity's concept of the feminine. He knew magic existed because it flowed through his veins, and he could see it with his own eyes.

Touching Morgan, tasting Morgan, was like watching the sunrise. Warmth spread throughout him, thawing the deep recesses of his soul that had never expected to receive light. Feeling her climax while he was at the center of her was what he imagined the Big Bang was like.

There was nothing for him to hold onto as the universe exploded around him. He felt himself expand, come apart at the seams. He was flung far and wide to an abyss where he could see nothing, only feel. It was frightening, terrifying. And he couldn't wait to do it again.

When the embers of their passion cooled, Arthur felt he had a new lease on life. Mankind had once believed the sun to revolve around the Earth. Opening his eyes, Arthur came out of the dark ages. The light of his world lay beneath him.

Morgan's eyes were closed as the tremors slowly

subsided. Her nails dug into his skin, anchoring him close to her. She needn't have worried that he'd ever leave her orbit.

Was this love?

Arthur wanted Morgan near him, to protect her, to kiss her, to touch her.

He wanted to hunt a beast, kill it, and feed her the choicest pieces of its flesh.

He wanted to spill his seed in her again and again. He ached to see her lush body swell with his child.

Was this love?

"Go on," she whispered. "Say it."

Those fire blue eyes bored into him. Arthur was tongue-tied. His heart raced.

She knew.

She knew that he was in love with her. He'd never felt so vulnerable in his entire life. And yet, even in this defenseless state, he knew with certainty that he'd give her his sword to do with him as she saw fit.

Love was madness.

"Say I told you so," Morgan said.

That was not what he wanted to say.

"You were right. It didn't hurt."

And then she smiled. That same smile filled with

pure joy and delight that he'd seen cross her face days ago when she was in the kitchen with Igraine. That's when Arthur knew for certain exactly what it was that he was feeling and exactly what it was called.

He pulled her close, placing a gentle kiss at the corner of her mouth, tasting her sweet joy. He wanted more, but what he'd taken, what they'd shared, would tide him over. For now.

"I told you," he said. "I will never hurt you. Raise my voice at you—most definitely. Try to intimidate you with my size—most likely. Dazzle you with my charisma and prowess—every moment of our lives. But never pain. I promise you that."

"Wow," she said snuggling into his chest as though she intended to stay forever. "It never felt so good to be proven wrong."

The sun streamed in announcing the new day. The rays flickered and danced, urging Morgan's eyes open. The stream of light was both particle and wave, like ice cubes melting and solidifying before her eyes. Morgan held her breath and watched, saw particles in the light stream.

Was this the residual effect of the hart? Or maybe it was a side effect of Arthur's lovemaking?

Morgan knew a woman wasn't supposed to feel any different after losing her virginity. It was a simple physiological event. But she felt different. She was seeing things differently. That warmth in her belly hadn't cooled, it burned in her gut. Nearly as bright as when she'd had her magic.

Maybe Arthur's penis was magic? There were a

number of romance novels out there that purported it was possible. Scientifically speaking, spermatozoa was a natural anti-depressant and a multi-vitamin containing melatonin, Vitamin C, calcium, and magnesium to name a few.

She hadn't consumed Arthur's seed. Though she knew that was done. Would Arthur want her to do that to him at some point? He had taken her sex into his mouth. Turnabout was fair play.

But no. That's not why Morgan was feeling so warm in her belly. It had to be because of Arthur's hand resting possessively on her abdomen.

She shifted, turning on her side so that she could see him. Immediately, his hold tightened, stoking the flames within her. It could've been the heat rolling off her body, or the shift in her position that woke him. Arthur's eyes sprang open. His gaze narrowed at her, accusingly.

"I'm not trying to escape," she said. "Just shifting positions."

Arthur sighed as though put out. He pressed a kiss to her temple and then released her. But his hold only opened enough for her to shift closer to him. Then he recaptured her in his arms, pulling her flush into his solid, hard body.

Morgan stole a glance down between their

bodies. The muscles in Arthur's thighs and ass flexed as he wrapped a leg over hers. She caught only a glimpse of that taut appendage between his thighs. What she couldn't see, she could most certainly feel.

"Keep looking at me like that," Arthur said, "and I will do something about it."

"We can't do anything about it again. Not now at least. I need to sneak out of here and get back to my room before anyone notices I'm gone."

"Sneak?" Arthur reached around her neck and gathered her nape in his palm. He gave a light but firm tug so that she tilted her head back to look at him. "From your husband's bed?"

"You're not my husband yet."

"I gave you my vow, Morgan."

The words he'd said to her last night came back to her. Her mind had been so fogged that she hadn't really been paying attention. But now she remembered.

She'd heard those words before. They were the Celtic vows of marriage. He'd said them to her while he was on his knees. As far as the old laws were concerned, they were bonded as man and wife.

"I told you," he said. "There's no going back. Your

things will be out of your room and in here, in our room, before lunch."

Morgan's hand came to rest on his strong chest. Her fingertips brushed roughened skin where he'd nearly lost his heart for her twice. His heartbeat was steady and strong. It kicked up at her touch.

"I'm not going back," she said.

Arthur's hand slid down her back. It came to rest at the curve of her ass as he pulled her thigh higher up over his.

"But I do want to talk about moving forward," she said. "I'm not going to take the fellowship."

He growled his assent as he bit at her neck.

"They're looking for Element 119. As we saw last night, that element is pure magic. I can't reveal that to the human world."

"No, you can't," Arthur agreed after tasting her collarbone. But then he paused and lifted his head. "Could they find it on their own?"

Morgan inhaled and then let out a slow breath. "Simon, that's the physicist I've been working with, he is quite brilliant. But he's going about his search the wrong way. They probably would've found it using my theory. Without me? It's possible. But not for a few years at best."

"Good. Magic in the hands of humans is dangerous."

Morgan didn't entirely agree with him. Not every human was out to burn witches at the stake. Many of their inventions and discoveries added creature comforts to the townsfolk here in Camelot.

"So, you'll take your role as Lady of the Castle?" he asked as he rested an elbow beside her head and peered down at her.

"No," said Morgan. "That's still Gwin's role. She's still married to the eldest Pendragon. She's better at it than I'd ever be. And you know it."

He neither conceded nor disagreed. "What will you do with yourself then? Before you answer that, know that I plan to take up a majority of your time at night ..." He kissed her shoulder. "At dawn ..." He kissed the top of her breast. "And pull you into dark halls at odd times during the day." He captured her lips with a searing kiss.

"But," he said after pulling away to peer down at her again, "I know you need something for yourself. Something without controlled substances and children would be preferable."

"I don't know," said Morgan. "I've always wanted to go to university, but I see now it's not the place for me. I'm back to being between the world of magic and science. Not many people live on this island. But I have time to figure it out. I have a wedding to plan. You're helping, by the way. If I have to postpone my career, you're staying at my side to plan this fiasco."

"And so the nagging begins." He rolled away, flopping back onto the mattress.

Morgan rolled on top of him and punched him in the arm. He gripped his arm as though her love tap had done true damage. She used the momentary distraction to slip out of his hold.

"Where are you going?" he growled as he reached for her with lightning quick reflexes. Luckily for her, she was just beyond his grasp.

"To get dressed." She slipped on her robe to his look of pure mutiny. "I have to go to the university."

"Didn't we just discuss how you're not taking the fellowship? Can't you snap or kick a message over the internet?"

"I need to tell Simon face to face."

"Simon?" Arthur spat out in a whiny, singsong voice.

"Things happened between us last night."

All humor left his voice "Things?"

"We nearly kissed."

Arthur swung out of the bed.

Morgan held up her hands before Arthur could

start. "But I stopped it. Because I realized I had feelings for someone else."

That caught his attention. "Feelings? What kind of feelings."

Morgan swallowed. "I'm still examining them."

She would not be the first to say those three words. Though she was very certain that they were what she felt. That's what the thing was. There was no other logical explanation for it.

"Simon and I made sense," she said by way of evasion. "But I'm coming to see that matters of the heart don't follow the laws of physics."

Arthur captured her in an embrace. His hold was loose, but she knew it was a false sense of freedom. He was not about to let her go.

"I don't have feelings for Simon. But I do have respect for him. He stuck his neck out on a limb for me. The least I can do is turn him down face to face."

"Fine. I'll come with you."

"You will not. I'm a big girl. I can do this myself."

"He's a man."

"I'm a witch. A non-practicing one, true. But I'm also a Galahad girl. Do you really think I can't handle a human scientist?"

Arthur gave her the look. It was the look he'd aimed at all three Galahad girls when he suspected them of something. It never worked on Morgan. That included now, even after he'd made her shake and tremble. He probably should've tried to kiss her silly. That would've likely gotten her to mind. But he hadn't gone that route. And she had no intention of directing him in this case.

"It won't take long," she said. "I'll drive in and be back—"

"Drive? Have Gwin open a ley line."

"You're being controlling. It will only take a couple of hours. Then I'll be back at your beck and call."

Arthur snorted, eyeing her with suspicion. "Do you want to know what I think? I think you just want another look at that lab."

Morgan didn't hide her grin. He knew her so well. She did want a final look at the cyclotron and a chance to say goodbye to the scientific world.

At least for now. This wasn't a farewell forever. Just a see ya later. Because she'd found the answer to the problem she was looking for. She'd found it in the least of all expected places; right here in her own backyard.

CHAPTER TWENTY-FIVE

*A*rthur walked hand in hand with his bride down the long and winding stair. It was late morning, nearly afternoon. He'd kept them in bed past breakfast just as he'd warned her. Now, he was eying the dark corner at the end of the hall. But that would have to wait.

The people of the town smiled as they walked by. Men nodded at him. Women giggled and whispered behind their hands. It was as Morgan had feared. Everyone knew what they had been up to. They'd missed dinner and breakfast, after all.

In response, Morgan simply raised an eyebrow as she curled her fingers around his. Good thing, because Arthur was having trouble keeping the lion-wide grin off his face.

No one scolded them for anticipating their vows. As far as he was concerned, they were wedded now. He'd given his vow and there were no take backs. Not ever. Arthur pressed a kiss to her temple, quelling the urge to throw her over his shoulder and carry her back to his bed.

Duty called. He needed to get to the Throne Room for his meeting with the knights. Up ahead, he saw Gwin talking with Brendan, the chimney sweep.

"I should've warned you," said Gwin. "We had a mishap a few days ago."

"I only had to clear out the flues in the east and west halls," said Brendan. "This one was like brand new on the interior. Whatever magic you used to clean it, bottle it up and sell it. I've never seen a flue sparkle like this."

Morgan lifted her head proudly as they walked by. "Like I said, a little vinegar will clean just about any situation. Or destroy the inner workings. It's either a blessing or a curse."

"Just like you," said Arthur.

Morgan punched him in the arm. He caught her closed fist in his before it could do any real or playful damage. Arthur unfurled her fingers and placed a kiss in her palm, darting his tongue out for a taste of her.

Morgan gasped. Her breasts rose and she arched towards him. Arthur pulled her to him and stole into her mouth.

"I have to go," she said when he allowed her up for a breath of air.

They were at the entryway of Tintagel. The door was wide open. A breeze of spring air sailed through with a slight hint of the last vestiges of winter. It was enough to bring Arthur to his senses.

"Don't dally," he said, letting Morgan go.

She frowned. "Just because I said I'd spend the rest of my life with you doesn't make you the boss of me."

"Don't. Dally." He leaned into her, using his size to intimidate. Of course, she wasn't cowed. "Because I have plans for you when you return."

He leaned into her ear and whispered all the carnal plans he had in store for when she returned home.

Morgan nodded, as though he were giving her a honey-do list. The only thing that betrayed her arousal was the quickness of her shallow breaths. And also the curl of steam he imagined rising from the top of her head.

"Those are very valid points," she said when he was done with his long list. "I will endeavor to return as soon as possible to help you with that."

"Good girl."

"And Arthur ..." She tugged her lower lip into her mouth. The move tried Arthur's resolve to not pull her into that dark hallway. "Thanks for not going caveman on me and demanding to drive me there so you can rip Dr. Accolon's head off."

"I'm a Renaissance man. Well, I was born during that time."

He gave her another peck on the lips before he finally released his hold on her. Arthur watched the sway of Morgan's hips without shame as she walked away from him. Then he watched as the squire ducked from behind the castle and set out on her trail. Before he did, the young squire turned and nodded to Arthur.

Arthur nodded in return. He may have been an enlightened man, but he wasn't born during the dark ages. A little added protection wouldn't hurt her. Especially if she didn't know about it.

Arthur turned back into the castle and headed into the Throne Room. Lance, Percy, and Tristan were already seated, going over documents instead of looking at electronics.

Bors sat with his arms crossed over his shoulders. He reminded Arthur of a child on Christmas who'd gotten a generic gift instead of the name brand he'd written to Santa about. Bors looked up when he saw Arthur. Their gazes held. After a moment, Bors nodded. Arthur knew the elder knight might not agree with his choice of bride, but Arthur was also the Lord of the Castle and Bors would respect his decision.

Once Arthur took his seat, the meeting began. But for once, Arthur had trouble keeping his attention on the matters of the day. He was always attentive at the roundtable meetings. But this morning he had thoughts of a dark-haired witch on his mind.

Morgan should be back in a few hours. Just enough time to finish this meeting, check in on the squires' training, and make his rounds around the town. Then he'd spend the rest of the day attending to his bride's plentiful rounds. She was due for some more stretching before their wedding night.

But for now, he snapped back to focus on his job. It would appear that his full attention was needed as the knight's dossier filled with events that needed his attention.

Lance had received word from Dame Loren.

Apparently, she had started a civil war amongst the Valkyrie sisters of Asgard. Arthur would've expected to be hearing from their father, Odin, but apparently, the god was off again on his travels.

If that weren't enough, a missive had been received from the fae king, Gyges. Geraint and Gawain had angered the trickster king when they ran off with a faerie princess who just happened to be Gyges's daughter.

For weeks Arthur had been craving action. Now that he craved peace to spend with this new bride, everything under the sun in this realm and a few of the others were coming to him at once. And if that wasn't enough the Templars appeared to be rearing their bloody heads again.

"I've received more information on the one who calls himself Malegant," said Percy. "There appears to be a connection between the Philosopher's Stone and the Friday, the 13th Massacre."

"Do you mean Harry Potter and Jason?" said Tristan.

"The Friday Massacre from the 14th century in France," said Lance. "When the king and the pope rounded up the Knights Templar and had them murdered."

"I know. It was a joke," said Tristan. "One Loren would've made if she were here."

Loren might have made the joke, but she might not have known the history. That massacre, which did happen to fall on Friday the 13th, had been a turning point in both human and magical history.

The original order of the Poor Fellow-Soldiers of Christ and the Temple of Solomon was better known as the Knights Templar. They had been formed by Hugues de Payens, the descendant of a witch. Hugues was also an ancestor of Arthur.

He had formed the Templars to escort the followers of Christ, which included his family of witches and wizards, to the Holy Lands. The Templars had carried out this mission for decades, and at some point, became increasingly wealthy in their mission.

By the turn of the 14th century their wealth caused envy and suspicion in the French King Philip IV and Pope Clement V. On Friday, October 13, 1307, hundreds of Templars across the land were rounded up and arrested. The hangings, burnings, and executions came soon after.

The world lost thousands of devout soldiers in the war against magic. Those Templars that remained turned to the church and broke with the Knights of Camelot. That's when the Templars began hunting knights and witches and snuffing out anything they deemed magical and therefore sinful.

"From my reports," said Percy, "this Malegant is planning to raise an army of the five hundred fallen."

"The fallen Templar Knights from the 14th century?" asked Tristan. "But they're dead."

"There is no magic that can raise the dead," said Lance. "This is a dead end. This Accolon or Malegant or whatever he calls himself—"

"Wait," said Arthur. "Say that again."

"Which part?"

"His name."

"He calls himself Malegant. His surname is Accolon."

The prickles started down Arthur's arm. Accolon wasn't a common name. But he didn't believe in coincidences.

"This is the man who married a Banduri?" said Arthur.

"Yes, but they divorced decades ago," said Percy. "They had one child. Grew up to be a physicist. Works at Cardiff University. Gained some notoriety as he's looking for a new element on the Periodic Table. His name is—"

But Arthur didn't need his name. He was already up and out of his chair.

CHAPTER TWENTY-SIX

Apparently, there had been a late-season snowstorm last night. Morgan hadn't noticed. How could she have? She'd been in a cocoon of warmth in Arthur's bed.

This afternoon, the roads were clear of the snowstorm. Mounds were shoved aside. Morgan heard the gravel of salt crunching under the tires.

There weren't many people on the highway, making her trip quick and easy. Even when she came to the city streets, cars turned in opposite directions from where she wanted to go. Lights turned green only seconds after turning red. It was like magic.

And because the roads were so clear and traffic so light, Morgan could clearly tell that she was being followed. She didn't panic. The car was familiar. It was from her town.

She very nearly picked up her cellphone to call Arthur and have it out with him. But, one, he'd likely chide her for using the phone while driving. And, two, she much preferred to confront him face to face upon her return.

Renaissance man, her ass.

Morgan pulled up to the campus. It was packed this afternoon. But before she began to crawl the lot for a spot, a car at the edge of the science building pulled out offering up its spot. If she didn't know any better, she'd say it was magic.

Too bad for her tail. They'd be searching for a spot for at least a good quarter hour if they were lucky. Then they'd have to hoof it across campus back to the science building before they could spy on her and report back to Arthur. Serves them right.

She couldn't believe Arthur didn't trust her. She could hear his argument now. It was only to protect you, would be his likely defense. Which was kinda cute.

Morgan shook her head. For decades, she'd hated having a gang of protectors. But something was different now that she had one that was her very own. Her anger was slipping further and further away as she walked into the science building.

She waved to the guard as she walked up to the gate. Pulling out her lanyard, she tapped the keypad. It gave a cheery beep as she made her final entrance.

Morgan waited for the nostalgia to hit her, but it didn't. This place wasn't where she belonged. These weren't her people.

Stepping off the elevator on the lab floor, she nearly collided with another person. A man in a dark jumpsuit stopped her just before she walked into a bucket filled with dirty water.

"My apologies," said the janitor. "I didn't see you there."

Morgan opened her mouth to accept his apology, but immediately closed it again. And then closed her eyes as well as the acidity of the cleaning products burned her throat and eyes.

"I see you took my advice about the vinegar," she said.

The old man's grin was huge. "It got these floors sparkling like nothing I've ever seen."

Morgan would've stayed and chatted with the man. But the watering in her eyes and the sting in her nostrils prevented it. She suspected the man may have gone overboard in his use of the acidic component. She managed a smile and a nod and then made her way past the janitor and into the lab.

Once inside, she felt the first pang of nostalgia. Looking up at the cyclotron and its wires and gears and lights, she had the first moment of doubt.

This was what she longed for; new discoveries, testing ideas, outlining variables, measuring results. But she already knew the outcome and she couldn't share the conclusion.

She'd assumed the accelerator would tell her secrets of the world that she couldn't see. In a way it had. She'd looked outside herself only to see that the answers had been inside of her all along.

Like a fox consuming a rooster to distill the truth. It all came back to alchemy. The secret was within you.

Morgan smirked. When had she become so cliché?

She turned from the accelerator. It wouldn't help her on the next part of her journey. The scientists in these halls couldn't accompany her on that path.

Morgan turned and saw Simon in the control room, a pencil between his lips, documents in his hands. His eyes scanned the data back and forth.

In another life, they'd have made great partners. As colleagues, definitely. Maybe even intimately.

Simon's instincts were spot on. She wished she could give him the final piece of the puzzle he wanted to solve. But she had pointed him in the right direction. The rest would be up to him. Though if he found the truth, would anyone in the scientific community even believe him?

Simon looked up as she came in. Then he frowned. "You don't have good news for me, do you?"

"I'm not taking the fellowship."

"Is it about what happened between us? Because I can assure you that, though I do have an attraction to you, I will be everything professional."

"No, it's not us. There can't be an us intimately or academically. Things have changed at home. I'm getting married."

"You're getting married?" The papers fell from his hands, fanning out in an interesting pattern. Most of the pages fell onto the control board. But one page was hanging on only by a corner.

"It was not my intention to waste your intellectual time," said Morgan. "Nor toy with your emotions. I thought this was what I wanted, what I needed to do with my life. And in a way, it was. I needed to test this theory. I just never thought it would come to this conclusion. You ever have that happen in a research project?"

"I have," said Simon. "It was with you, in fact. You were not what I expected."

The lone sheath of paper fell to the floor. But not quick. It floated down, taking its time on the current of air. When it impacted the ground, there was no sound. The lack of a thud further increased the awkwardness of the moment between Morgan and Simon.

A squeak, a clang, and metallic bang sounded in the other room. Both Morgan and Simon's gaze immediately went to the control panel. But it was dim and quiet. They lifted their heads to the cyclotron. The door had opened and the janitor had wheeled in his bucket of acidic water.

"You can't have those cleaning products in here," Simon shouted. He rushed past Morgan with his hands outstretched.

The janitor jerked to attention. The bucket making another creaking sound. The water sloshing to the sides of the pail with the janitor's movement.

"Sorry, boss," said the janitor. "It's my first week. I'll get it out of here."

The man made to step out of the room, but the wheel of the bucket stuck. He gave it a jerk and the water tipped up nearing the top of the rim.

The acid smell hit Morgan's nose again. She

turned and saw the look of sheer horror on Simon's face. If those chemicals got close to the cyclotron, the accelerator would malfunction. All his work would be lost.

Morgan didn't want to be on the scientific team any longer. But she couldn't have such an amazing piece of equipment damaged. But what could she do? She couldn't get to the bucket in time.

The water sloshed against the other side of the pail. Up higher this time, and then over the top. Morgan felt the fire rage in her belly. She threw out her hands.

The water sloshed back into the bucket. Not up against the other side. It settled down into the belly of the pail and stilled.

All was still inside the room. The janitor ceased his attempts to yank the wheel into motion. Simon had stilled in his advance. And Morgan stood, with her hands outstretched, palms burning.

That's when the accelerator alarm blared, announcing that there had been a hit.

"I'm so sorry," said the janitor. "I'll just grab some towels to get this up."

His eyes were wide on the machine as he backed out of the room. He likely thought the alarm had been caused by his clumsiness. But there wasn't any spilled liquid on the floor. The pail and the water sat still and whole in front of the lab's door.

Morgan stared down at her hands. The alarm screeched in her ears. Her hands were on fire—with witch fire. Her gut burned and she realized, it wasn't love she felt there. It was magic.

Last night, when the hart had healed Arthur, it had healed her too. Her powers were back. She wanted to jump and shout for joy.

She looked up to find Simon. Instead of running to the control panel to examine the readings, Simon stared at her with that same wide-eyed, covetous expression that Arthur had turned on her this morning. Only there was no heat of desire in Simon's gaze.

"All my life, I wasn't a believer, and then came you," said Simon. "I've never questioned so much since the day you came into my life. I've gone back and forth over what I was taught as a child, and what I believed as a learned man. And now, even seeing it with my own eyes, I still have trouble believing the truth."

"The truth?" said Morgan. "What truth?"

"You're a rooster rising at dawn, my lady. There's pure gold inside you."

Morgan looked down again at her blazing hands.

She should extinguish this magical fire in front of a human. But it was already too late. She couldn't make Simon unsee what he was seeing. Not without a memory potion. Arthur was going to be pissed.

"I want you to know that I'm not doing this for my father," said Simon.

"Your father? Doing what?" Morgan had lost the track of the conversation as she tried to get her magic under control.

"This is for science. Just as the ancient alchemists believed you could distill gold using acid and recreate it."

"Simon, what are you talking about?"

"I'm sorry, Morgan. But I'm going to have to feed you to the fox."

Morgan frowned. He wasn't making any sense. Was he talking about the Red Dragon painting? But why? And then too late, she realized his intentions.

Simon reached out and pushed Morgan into the circle of the particle accelerator.

CHAPTER TWENTY-SEVEN

Arthur rushed into the ley line opened by Gwin. He barely heard Lance's admonishments to Gwin about staying behind. It was her sister that was in danger. But Morgan was more than Gwin's sister, she was Arthur's everything.

When had that happened?

He didn't want to face the sun without her. His bed would be an empty hole at night unless she was beside him. His heart ached, as though his wound had been ripped open and cut deeper at the thought of any harm coming to her.

He told himself to calm down. He'd sent a squire in after her. One of his best. Squires were trained to handle this very case. But Arthur wanted—no, needed—to undertake this quest himself.

He wished he could run through the ley line. But he had to maintain stillness as the magic worked around him. The inter-dimensional travel would take him twenty miles in seconds.

It wasn't fast enough. Every worst thing imaginable rushed through Arthur's head in the first five seconds it took to travel the line. What if it was too late? What if Morgan was already hurt? What if she needed him right now and he wasn't there for her?

Finally, the trip through the magical highway ended and let him out on the other end. Most ley lines were made over holy places. Devotion created a special brand of energy that gathered and coalesced into pockets that made magic.

Arthur opened the door of the Cardiff University campus chapel. His boots ate up the distance of the pews. He startled the devoted during midday devotion.

Without waiting to see if Lance was behind him, Arthur ran through the courtyard. He drew his sword at cosplayers when he saw a dark-haired woman in someone's grasp. But when Excalibur sliced the wooden sword into kindling, Arthur realized his mistake.

He growled his frustration at the frightened

humans. Frantic, he looked around at the buildings. They all looked exactly alike to him.

But then he felt it. A jolt, a shock of energy. He took off in that direction.

He looked up and read the name of the building that called to him. Science Department. This had to be it.

He reached the door the same time as the squire he'd sent after Morgan reached the door. The squire looked shocked to see Arthur there. Arthur didn't waste time listening to any excuses, he shot through the doorway. The squire and Lance were on his heels.

Arthur shoved aside the guard who came to stand at the entrance. The lord of Camelot wrapped his palm around the man's neck demanding to be let into the elevator. In fear for his life, the man acquiesced and even pushed the button where the lab was located.

Arthur chided himself for not taking the stairs when the elevator took ten full seconds to ascend. Finally, the doors opened and he leaped out, brandishing his sword and shouting Morgan's name.

He burst into the lab and his heart settled. There she was. Standing in the center of the room under a fluorescent spotlight. She was whole, fine.

And then she doubled over.

Her features contorted in pain as beams of light fired all around her. The first beam hit her and brought her to her knees. More beams fired, largely missing her. But Arthur could see that it was only a matter of time before another hit its mark. He had to get to her.

He stormed in and was immediately brought to his knees. He looked up to see a tall, slight man looming over him. In his hand, he held a stone.

"My apologies for this," said the man, the younger Accolon.

There was an open locket made of lead around his neck. That's where Arthur assumed the stone had come from. Lead was the only metal that muted the sickening powers of a sarsen stone.

"I do truly abhor violence. That disappointed my father. But my mother prepared me."

A Templar Knight would've taken a blade to a Knight of Camelot. Honor demanded it. Sarsen stones were the weapons of the Banduri priestesses. If ever there would be an ounce of respect for this ill-bred mutt of a Templar and Banduri, it was decimated.

"You know that the Banduri have struck a treaty with Camelot," said Arthur. It was a struggle to speak under the weight of the thumb-sized stone. "I consider you holding my bride hostage a clear breach of that treaty."

Accolon nodded. "I do regret that. The lady is truly a prize. Not just her beauty, but her brains. She's quite brilliant, you know."

"Of course I know," growled Arthur.

"If you did, you wouldn't have neglected her."

Arthur tried to inch closer, but the stone was too much for him. "Fine. I'll repent my sins. Let her go if your quarrel is with me."

"This has nothing to do with you." The man reached down for a trash pail. He emptied the contents and then set the stone atop the upended bin, just beyond Arthur's reach.

"I suppose it has to do with your father then?" said Arthur as he eyed the stone and then the man with contempt.

"If you know about my father, then you know he's been searching for the Philosopher's Stone all his life."

"There's no such thing."

"I'd beg to differ, but I've seen enough movies. I know that while I give the villain speech you're only stalling, looking for a way to get out of my dastardly plan. The problem is, I'm not the villain here."

With the stone balanced on the bin, Accolon stood and went to the side room. Arthur could see him pressing buttons and gathering documents. Inside the lit circle, the beams continued firing around Morgan.

"Science has triumphed today," said Accolon. "Thanks to the lady, I've found Element 119. I had the suspicion that the only thing that could hold all of those charges together was beyond the known substances. And I was right. I just didn't think it would be magic."

Accolon turned to Morgan. He looked at her in wonder as she stood trapped inside the circle as a giant beam of light fired all around her. The beam missed her again and again, but Arthur knew that soon it would strike her body.

"As soon as I extract the element from her body, I can make it synthetically. Synthetic magic. My name will go down in history alongside Einstein, Newton, Hawkins."

Arthur wasn't listening. He was stuck on *extract it from her body.* Just then a beam of light pulsed inside the circle and hit Morgan square in the chest. Morgan screamed. The sound pierced Arthur's ears and struck into his heart to lodge into his soul.

"I am sorry, Morgan," said Accolon. "But you

would be thrilled at these readouts. I will give you credit on the paper, posthumously. As I told you, I'm not a sexist."

Arthur made another push to move for her. He barely got an inch. Their eyes connected as they both were doubled over on the floor. But Morgan's eyes went past him, looking over his shoulder.

All his strength and he was being felled by a stone.

He'd been gutted by a stag. He'd been brought to his knees by this woman of science. Now, he couldn't raise his sword over a stupid stone.

There had to be some way. He just needed to think. But his brain fogged as the smell of acid burned his nose and reddened his eyes.

"You must understand," Accolon was saying. He was at the console tapping on keys. "I don't hate witches like my mother. I don't want to kill knights like my father. I don't care about any ancient feud. It's all about the science for me. Morgan will understand. She is a woman of science."

Morgan's gaze connected with Arthur's. Her blue eyes flashed fire. There was pain there, but there was also ... calculation.

Arthur wanted to growl his ire. But then he realized; Accolon was right. His bride was a woman of science. He could see her beautiful mind at work.

She wasn't looking over his shoulder at someone. She was looking at something. Arthur turned his head. His foot was near a bucket of dirty mop water. He realized that was the source of the smell.

She was brilliant.

Arthur moved his sword out of the way. Once again, it was useless in this particular battle. He stretched out his foot and kicked over the bucket of dirty water.

The acid-laced water spilled. The water caused the trash bin to sail on its lower current, sending the stone on a slow trek out of the door. But that wasn't all. The corrosive water flowed upstream as well, directly into the path of the machine.

From the other room, Arthur heard Accolon shout. But it was too late. The water spilled into the circle and the beam of lights flickered off.

Morgan collapsed to the ground, but not before raising her palm. With the stone out of play, Arthur struggled to his feet. When he did, he was met with steel. The stone wasn't the only weapon Accolon had up his sleeve. He also had a gun in his pocket apparently. The barrel of the gun was pointed at Arthur.

"Let me have her," said Accolon. "This is my life's work. She's one witch. You have others."

"She is my life," said Arthur, pressing his chest into the barrel of the gun.

The two knights came to Arthur's back. Accolon's gaze flicked to them. The man had to know that even if he pulled that trigger, his life was forfeited.

The scientist turned out to be a smart man. He hung his head. He made a motion to indicate he was handing the gun over. But before he relinquished the weapon, an alarm blared through the room and everything went wrong.

The knights rushed forward at the alarm. Accolon's body jerked at the sound, causing his finger to pull the trigger. The blast tore through the room causing Arthur's body to jerk. The last thing Arthur saw was Morgan rushing toward him.

And then everything went black.

CHAPTER TWENTY-EIGHT

*P*ain ripped through Morgan. The beam hit her, burning her flesh with each impact. Her flesh tore, but instead of blood leaking out, she felt power being leeched from her soul like a battery being drained.

Her hands were luminescent. The witch fire burned bright, but she couldn't focus and aim it at anything with the beam constantly assaulting her.

She'd felt this pain before. She was reliving that nightmare. Only she was awake. When the Spear of Destiny had slashed through her skin and left her powerless. But she hadn't been powerless all these months.

She had her mind. She had a family who loved her. She had a man who was prepared to give his life for hers. But instead of giving up his life, Arthur listened to her.

He caught her gaze when she looked at the vinegar-filled mop bucket. He managed to kick the bucket. The sarsen stone floated away and out the door. The accelerator cranked to a halt. The beam went dark and the world stopped spinning. The pain stopped.

Morgan wanted to black out, but the loud bang after her freedom from the pain ripped her eyes open. The pain she'd felt as the beams blasted her paled in comparison to watching Arthur fall to the floor under the weight of another, smaller bit of metal.

He crumbled to the ground clutching at his heart. His eyes never left her on his descent.

Morgan vaguely heard Simon whimper. "It was an accident. I didn't mean to."

The knights surrounded the scientist, despite the shaking gun in his hand. But they didn't get a chance to put their hands on him.

Simon went flying into the air, landing with a sickening thud against the wall on the opposite side of the room.

Morgan lowered her hand. The magic she'd used

to displace Simon still crackled in her fingertips. She knelt before Arthur.

Blood dampened his tunic. His gaze was vacant. But he found her.

"I'm going to say it," he managed.

No. Now was not the time for romantic overtures. That could wait. He would survive this. He had to survive this.

"I told you so," he said. His voice reedy and thin.

"What?" said Morgan.

"Science and magic … mix them together … dangerous."

Not funny. Not even in the slightest bit funny.

Arthur coughed. A slight trickle of blood slipped on his lower lip. A lip she'd tasted just a few hours ago.

"I swear to God," she said, "if you die on me right now, I will never speak to you again."

His lip quirked up in a faint smile. The move must have been too much for him because his eyes closed. "I told you I'd give my life for you. I vowed it."

"If you're trying to get out of this engagement, it won't happen. You're stuck with me. Now open your eyes."

But he didn't. He let out a pained sigh and then

he said in a voice that was slipping further and further away. "Be a good girl, Morgan."

A small smile lit his lips and then his mouth went slack. His pulse weakened, slowing. Blood seeped out of the wound at his heart.

He was dying.

She looked up at the other knights. There were tears in Lance's eyes. The young squire who'd followed her here hugged his arms to himself, the blood drained from his face.

There was nothing they could do. Science couldn't heal a wound like this. There was no spell that could bring someone back from the dead.

Morgan knelt over him feeling powerless. Then she realized, she wasn't powerless. And Arthur wasn't dead.

Not yet. She could fix this. She knew how to fix this.

The hart had shown her how. He'd shown her the bonds that held the fabric of the universe together. That essence, that element, was inside her. She could use it to knit Arthur back together.

The hart had given its life to her. This had to be why. To save Arthur's life.

Morgan didn't think twice. She pressed her lips to Arthur's as she covered his heart with her hands.

Then she poured her very soul into the man she loved.

She watched as bursts of light swirled inside of him. Colliding, separating, repairing the old, forging something new.

This was more than magic. It was also science. She had to know what went where and how to put the man she loved back together. It wasn't her brain that guided her, it was her heart.

The damage was extensive. It was taking all of Morgan's energy to knit Arthur back together. She saw that her stores were depleting rapidly. She barely had any left for herself.

And so she did the only logical thing. She poured more of herself into Arthur. All of herself.

Light burned her eyelids. It was the light of truth. The answer to the one question she'd never considered. It all made sense now.

The answer; love was magical.

Morgan felt Arthur's arms come around her. She felt his lips warm and then return her kiss. She felt him sigh as the breath of life filled his lungs.

And then everything went black.

CHAPTER TWENTY-NINE

Arthur brushed Morgan's hair from her temple. Then he tangled his fingers in the dark locks. She was so beautiful. He'd never taken a moment to really look at her until the past few days. In the past, she'd always been a blur of motion and mischief.

She was still now. Had been for three days.

When they'd returned home from Cardiff, he'd moved her from the infirmary into his room – their room as soon as both Gwin and Igraine had diagnosed her as being in a magically induced coma and not in any physical danger. There was no telling when she would wake up. It could be a couple of days. It could be a couple of months. However long it took her body to heal.

Morgan shifted on the bed. She sighed, parting those beautiful lips. Her closed eyes twitched beneath the lids. But they didn't open. She maintained the same serene, peaceful look that she'd had for the last two days. But still, she didn't wake.

Arthur had sacrificed his life for her. It was his duty, his honor. In classic Morgan fashion, she didn't take the gesture lying down. She'd turned around and done the same for him. A war raged in his heart over whether to be angry or touched.

Most times he found himself in the middle of the war. He'd give his heart to have her open her eyes and glare at him. To deliver a biting, witty remark. To talk to him ad nauseam about atoms and constants.

But all he could do was lay down next to her each night. He held her close during the day, telling her his secrets, sharing his dreams for their life together.

He'd pull himself away from her in the late morning to handle his duties. He didn't stay away long. She was his main priority.

Arthur barely listened in the briefings. His mind was always back upstairs wondering if Morgan had moved, shifted, finally opened her eyes. He wanted to be there when she did, needed to. To let her know that she was safe. That that bastard, Accolon, was locked away in the dungeons.

But he also had to do the work to keep her safe. He sat wishing the current meeting was done. He wanted to get back to his room. Back to her.

He tried not to be impatient. He felt guilty that he was so full of energy while she lay still. This was the energy from her. He wished he could give it back to her.

In the meantime, he had another plan. A present for her for when she did wake up. Arthur climbed the stairs to a tower in the east wing of the castle. Once he'd come to the landing, he heard banging of nails and sawing of wood.

The laboratory he'd built for his bride was in a simple room. Cabinets and tables lined the walls. Atop the surfaces were an array of equipment from beakers to Bunsen burners. He'd even put up a whiteboard in front of chairs and desks so that she could teach those interested in the sciences.

In one corner, Annora Godfrey and Osbert Clarke had their heads together over a circular device. It was a tabletop particle accelerator.

Morgan wouldn't be able to do the in-depth research she'd been after back at the labs in Cardiff, and that was just fine with Arthur. He would never let her near another of the large monstrosities.

"Is this for me?" asked a smoky voice from behind him.

All work in the lab stopped. Everyone turned to the doorway, looking past Arthur. But Arthur was slow to turn around.

He'd been anticipating this moment for days. And now that it was finally here, his mind stopped working. He'd never have to look at her again and wonder if she'd wake up. He'd never have to barter with God to hear her voice. The wait was over.

The sun shone its spotlight on Morgan. Her olive-toned skin gleamed as though she'd been lying beneath its rays for days and not inside his room with the blinds drawn. Her red lips looked as though he'd been kissing her for hours. Her blue eyes were wide enough for him to fall into.

"Is this my wedding gift?" Morgan stood barefoot in the doorway, dressed in a robe with her sister at her back.

Arthur approached her carefully, as though he was terrified she'd spook and fall back into her slumber. But when he stepped up to her she didn't flee.

No. The only thing that moved were her lips.

They stretched into a smile, so bright his steps faltered. He nearly fell to her feet.

"You're awake," he said.

"You're alive," she said.

"You shouldn't be out of bed," he scolded.

Like always, she ignored him. "You're building me a lab?"

She tried to move past him, but he didn't let her go. She was warm and awake and alive.

Bodies began to file out of the room, squeezing past them with murmured well-wishes about her health. Morgan nodded but didn't take her eyes off the wonders in front of her.

"Do you like it?" Arthur asked once the room was clear.

Morgan squeed. High pitched and ear-splitting. It was the best sound Arthur had ever heard in his life.

"I love it. But not as much as I love you."

She beamed up at him. Her smile filled with enough joy to sucker punch him. But then she winced and groaned. Her head fell to her chest in disappointment.

What had he gotten wrong? Whatever it was, he'd fix it immediately. He needed this to be perfect for her.

"Crap," Morgan moaned. "I didn't want to be the first to say it."

"To say what?"

She huffed out a hot breath. "You know what. Those three little words. I wanted you to be the first to say it."

Arthur chuckled. Then he threw his head back and laughed. Then he gathered her tightly to him, leaving no space for escape.

"Say it again," he demanded.

"No. I gave you my soul. You can give me those three words."

"I took a bullet for you. Straight to the heart."

Morgan ran her hand over his heart. The scar from the hart and the bullet were still there. But once again, the wound had closed.

Hopefully, this would be the last time his heart took a beating. But he wouldn't hesitate to do it all again in the future for this woman in his arms. He loved her more than anything in this world.

"I love you," Morgan whispered.

"Again."

"I love—"

Arthur captured her lips. He tried to press his entire spirit into her. It wasn't hard. The two of them shared the same essence. Where he ended, she began. He knew it to be the truth because kissing Morgan, tasting her breath, feeling her heartbeat was a homecoming.

"You are my love," he said. "You are my life. You are truly the reason that my heart beats."

"Well, it's the blood pumping through your veins that's causing your heart to beat."

"Because you pushed your essence into me. We share the same soul now. You can't quantify how I feel about you."

"Yes, I can. Give me a second to do the math."

"It's magic, Morgan. Didn't we just learn that science and magic are not in opposition? They can coexist."

"Just like us."

"Just like us."

Gwin ushered the motley crew down the stairs from the nearly complete science lab. As her soft slippers touched the first stair, she heard a groaning creak. She paused on the step and added to her mental notes to get the repairman to check it out.

That list of mental notes was ever increasing with all the reconstructions and updates and makeovers necessary in this ancient castle. It was because of her diligence, and the diligence of all the Ladies of the Castle that came before her, that Tintagel Castle, this marvel of architecture and magic still stood proud centuries after its initial construction and many moves.

A crack rent the air when the toe of her shoe

touched down on the next step. Before her foot could slip inside the splintered wood, a hand was at her elbow lifting her to safety.

"Careful, my lady."

Lance's touch burned through the fabric of Gwin's sleeve. The heat of his touch spread through her like wildfire. It always did whenever they had occasion to touch, which was far too infrequent.

She looked up into his handsome face and her breath caught. There was that perpetual flame in his blue gaze. There was the spark in his golden irises that twinkled only for her. There was the flare of his nostrils whenever she came near.

His lips said *be careful*. His gaze spoke a different message. They were words never uttered in the English language. Nor in the Gaelic of his Scottish ancestors. Neither in the Celtic of her ancestors. But she understood him clearly, had since the first moment they'd laid eyes on each other.

You are the other half of my soul, was the unspoken utterance.

Simply being in your presence fuels me, was the unannounced transmission.

You are the dream I awaken to, came the muted revelation.

The moment stretched into forever in their silent

communication. Gwin tasted the spice of his breath as he exhaled. She smelled the familiar woodsy scent of him. She felt the coiled energy of him as they stood close, yet too far apart.

She felt the unique pattern of the pad of his index finger just at her elbow. She concentrated so hard with each of his touches that she would swear she knew the intricate impression of his fingerprint. His thumb only barely touched the outside of her elbow, but she knew it well too.

Though their touches were fleeting and infrequent Gwin had cataloged each one. Each one she cherished like the sacred gift that it was. The look in Lance's sparkling eyes, the slight rise of his lip into a secret smile, told her that he did the same.

"Isn't it so romantic," came Annora Godfrey's voice from behind them. "It must remind you of your proposal, Lady Gwin."

Lance jerked his hand away. The light in his eyes shuttered. That slight rise of his lip fell like a heavy stone in a fathomless pool of water.

"It was so long ago," said Gwin, trying to catch her breath at the sudden impact of the cold solitude left by Lance's withdrawal.

Lance made haste down the steps and away from her. Like always, Gwin swallowed down her disappointment over the one thing she'd ever wanted but could never have, and turned to face Annora with a smile plastered on her face. It was the Hostess Smile, as Morgan called it. The fake smile that hid her true feelings away from all but Morgan, and Lance.

"I'm going to have it all, just like you and your sister," said Annora. "A career and a husband who loves me."

The sound of Lance's footfalls on the creaky steps was silent. He was beyond Gwin's reach now. He'd never been within her reach, not even back on the day they'd met. The day she'd fallen in love for the first and only time in her life. She knew he'd felt it too. She'd seen it in his eyes, in his smile, before he opened his mouth and told her so. It was a secret they shared that would never see the light of day, or touch anyone else's ears.

Gwin held tight to her Hostess Smile as she continued on down the steps, leaving her sister and her fiancé to their own amorous devices. Though she supposed Arthur was truly Morgan's husband now. When Morgan opened her eyes the first thing she asked for was him. In the time it took the sisters to walk up the stairs to the lab, Morgan had told Gwin about the vows she and Arthur had exchanged the night of their engagement. Morgan had more than hinted at the other activities the two had gotten up to after the vows.

Just as Gwin had had no words for Morgan about her carnal activity, she had no words for Annora about proposals. Gwin had no experience of being proposed to. Her marriage had been arranged. She had no experience of a man saying ancient vows, Merlin had repeated after the priest while coughing through the entire ceremony.

Gwin had no experience of sneaking off for secret embraces with her betrothed. She hadn't even had that experience on her wedding night. She soon learned that her new husband's illness rendered him unable to perform his marital duties. She'd never known the touch of a man. Her marriage had never been consummated. If anyone ever found out, she'd lose her title, her position, and her place amongst her people.

Lady Gwin held her head high and held her smile in place as she descended the stair and moved amongst the people who depended on her. She may live in an enchanted castle, but she knew better than anyone that fairytales didn't always come true.

ABOUT THE AUTHOR

Lover of fairytales, folklore, and mythology, Ines Johnson spends her days reimagining the stories of old in a modern world. She writes books where damsels cause the distress, princesses wield swords, and moms save the world.

You can sign up for her mailing list and receive alerts and free reads at http://bit.ly/InesReaders.